GRAVEL SWITCH: THE BLACK GOAT CHRONICLES BOOK 1

A WEIRD TALE OF EXTREME HORROR

ALEISTER J. DAVIDSON

BLACK MANTIS PRESS LLC

Dedicated to Sandra Faye Davis.

Those who dream by day are cognizant of many things which escape those who dream only by night.

-Edgar Allan Poe

PROLOGUE

*L*ester and Betty were having an exciting day for a couple in their seventies living in the middle of nowhere, outside Perryville Kentucky. A young couple in their early thirties was coming to see them about an ad they had run online for a rental property. They both knew that they had already rented the house out to a writer and his wife, a schoolteacher. Still, they were willing to withhold that information from the young couple just for the chance to have some company.

Things moved very slowly in Marion County and something as uncommon as visitors less than half of one's age was a big deal to talk about. As she realized that she would be the talk of the town at her next BINGO game Betty prepared some sweet tea before the guests arrived as Lester went out to the toolshed to deal with a problem. It was a problem he couldn't be having when guests arrived.

Lester took a syringe and a medicine bottle of clear liquid with him out to the toolshed. He opened the door to see the fat, middle-aged man still hogtied on the floor. He was obviously exhausted and dehydrated but he somehow managed the strength to squirm in protest and scream through the gag that was in his mouth.

"Jesus, Phil. You stink to high heaven," the old man said as he wafted the air away from his nose. Phil had been left with no choice but to wallow in his own waste for the week that he had been left in the shed.

Lester stepped forward into the shed, uncapped the syringe then closed the door behind him. Phil continued to waste his energy, squirming and screaming. Lester forcefully stuck the needle into the fat man's leg, through his blue jeans.

"Now Phil, this here is a sedative. You're gonna be out for a while. After our visitors leave then I'll come back and check on you. If you've come to by then I'll bring you some food and water. Gotta fatten you up some more anyway buoy!" Lester said in his thick country accent, teasing Phil and poking at him.

Phil knew he had gotten himself in way over his head. He just prayed that the folks who were coming to visit were able to see through Lester and Betty and their kinfolk. Sure they seemed nice enough on the surface, but...Phil found the sedative working and his thoughts faded into obscure dreams as he slept in the hot shed, snoring loudly.

Lester heard Betty calling him from the back porch, "Company's here dear!"

The old man walked back to the house, leaving the syringe in the shed with Phil. He locked up with a combination padlock and prayed that Phil wouldn't wake up and make any noise while the visitors were on the property. The last thing he needed was some city folk to get offended and not understand what he was doing.

The old couple met the young couple on the front porch

like a modern American Gothic portrait. He was wearing a red flannel shirt and she had a serving tray with glasses of iced tea. "Welcome," they said in unison.

"Hi there," the wife said as she got out of the car. "I'm Amy Ramsey. This is my husband Hank." Her neutral accent didn't have anything of country life in it at all.

"Nice to meet you. I'm Lester and this is my wife Betty. Would you like some iced tea?" the old man asked as his wife lifted the tray up and took a few steps towards them. Both of the Ramseys were grateful to have a cold glass of tea, but Amy was quite shocked by how sweet it was.

"You guys are welcome to stay for dinner if you like, but I'm afraid that we have already rented the place you guys came all the way out here to look at," Betty said in a maternal way, trying not to disappoint them too hard.

Hank began to wonder why the couple couldn't have just told them. It was an hour and a half drive from where they lived in Lexington and he thought that the old couple had been quite rude not to have at least called them and let them know. They thought they were going to be looking at and possibly renting a new place to live that day. When Lester spoke though, Hank knew that he had judged them too soon.

"We have some friends just down the way in Gravel Switch that have a house near twice the size and its half as much. I heard they want to rent it, but it needs some work. They haven't had a tenant in twenty years. I will give you their number. I just talked to them last week and mentioned I was gonna rent my other property and they seemed really interested to do the same," Lester reassured them both. "You know why they call it Gravel Switch? Cuz that's where the road switches to gravel," the weathered old man broke out into laughter.

It was important to Hank to move out to the country. He

had been suffering from severe epilepsy for years. He had hit his head into the steering wheel, rear-ended in a car wreck, when working as a pizza delivery man. Ever since that fateful day he had been having seizures and he just wanted to live out in the middle of nowhere and relax. He didn't tell Lester and Betty that he intended to grow marijuana in the house, but he certainly didn't hesitate to take the number from them.

The four of them had a nice meal in the dining room of the little country home. Fried chicken, mashed potatoes, corn on the cob, greens with cornbread and salad. It was a veritable country feast and did as much to nourish the Ramseys emotionally as it did physically.

After dinner, the younger couple thanked the older for their hospitality and kindness profusely. They drove home back to Lexington feeling confident about the kind of people that they would meet in their new community. They talked about it all the way home as if the house that they hadn't even seen yet would be theirs. It excited them. They had seen Lester and Betty's house and it was more than enough for the two of them. A house twice the size would give them all sorts of opportunities.

Hank could get started growing his marijuana again. They had been shut down by the D.E.A. after getting raided years before and hadn't ever been able to reestablish their grow operation. The government raid had changed everything about their lives. There were many things that they had to do in order to remain free from prison. Things neither of them wanted to do nor ever thought they would be capable of doing. One of the sources of Hank's greatest anxiety was running into someone seeking retribution for the actions he had taken trying to keep himself and his wife from being locked up. And anxiety was one of the major contributors to Hank's seizures.

So the Ramseys saw no other choice than to move out to the middle of nowhere. Both to get away from their own conscience and to be in relaxing surroundings. They reasoned that if the house had been empty for twenty years then they should have no problem getting it. There obviously wasn't much of a demand for it. It mattered little to them if there was work to be done. Hank had done roofing as a teenager and he had plenty of friends in the construction business. And with that attitude, they returned home to Lexington for the last time.

THE LANDLORD AND THE HOUSE

*E*ven at first glance, Hank could tell the house was not typical in any way, shape or form. Sitting a quarter mile off of the main road, down a driveway partially gravel and partially dirt, it stood. A massive Queen Anne Victorian on a sprawling lot. Acre upon acre of fields, woodlands, rolling hills, ponds…this property had it all. Everything he imagined that would relax his stressed-out mind when he set his sights upon greener pastures and decided leaving the city was in his cards. Hank was a simple man and he had simple pleasures. This slice of heaven would do for his purposes just fine. He wondered what was going through Amy's head as they approached the giant house. Was she as impressed as he was? If so it did not show on her face? In fact, there was nothing but distress showing on her face. She was doing her best to hide it, but he knew that look too well.

Before they had traveled down the entirety of the driveway Hank knew Amy's superstitious side was getting the best of her. The place certainly did look the part of a demon house from some half-baked, nineteen eighties, low budget horror movie. He chuckled a little to himself as they got to the end of the driveway. She smacked his arm with her purse and shot him a dirty look, knowing that he was amused by her obvious fear.

This was it. The place they had been looking for. A large house, out in the middle of nowhere, where they could relax and grow their signature strain of marijuana undisturbed by anyone or anything. On the phone, the landlord said the property rented for all of $300 a month, which Hank found to be much more disturbing than the look of the house itself. "With any deal this good there is always a catch," he thought. "I wonder what is wrong with the place?" He got out of the car and stretched his legs, took a deep inhale of the country air and began to laugh hysterically.

"Amy, I think this is it! We've found our new home! After looking for months, we've found our home and it is perfect," he said with a boyish tone that revealed he was truly in a state of wondrous, joyful bliss.

"Don't get too excited Hank," Amy deadpanned as she batted her eyelashes at him, trying to remind him that she also had a say in the situation. "We haven't even seen the inside yet. And we haven't met the landlord either. What if he's some sort of psycho-freakazoid or some kind of inbred, hillbilly retard? I don't know if I've ever even been this deep out in the country before; this remote. What if they're all Deliverance-y?" She jokingly began to make pig noises at Hank, mocking him back for the way he had treated her on the way down the driveway.

"My god Amy…you never stop do you?" he began to speak with an authoritative tone to let her know they were about to bicker. He stopped himself when a vehicle appeared on the road and began down the driveway toward them. It was an old pickup truck that looked, much as the house did, like a relic of a bygone age. It putted down the driveway at a crawl and at first, had appeared to be a dark brown but as it approached revealed itself to be solid rust. The Ramsey's were both intrigued by it and wondered how it was still running and what make and model it was.

"Well, here he is now Hank. Guess we're about to see…"

The truck came to a stop next to their Subaru Outback, sputtering to a halt and spewing out clouds of steam from under the hood. Dust seemed to kick up around it just for the hell of it. Out of the truck stepped a woman in her mid-thirties. Dark haired and athletically built she carried herself with a confidence that left Hank and Amy immediately wondering if she drove cattle or rode bucking broncos in the rodeo. She was dressed in riding boots and jeans and wore an Almann Brothers Band t-shirt.

"Hi there. You must be Hank and Amy. I'm Bernice. Bernice Hickman. But you can call me Bernie. All my friends do," she said in a thick country accent that they both found endearing and comforting. There was something nurturing and maternal in her voice, even though she was only a few years older than they were.

"That's us," Amy said before Hank could answer. "Nice to meet you."

"Oh, you too Honey. Now let me show you around," Bernice said as she looked through her key ring for the keys to the house.

Bernice walked across the yard, from the driveway to the front porch. To Hank, it seemed to take forever as the front yard alone was several acres. The stairs to the front porch left Hank feeling quite small but he followed her and Amy was close behind him.

"Look at the huge porch Hank!" Amy said excitedly. Hank

was spacing out, paying more attention to the peeling paint, which showed the age of the house. He experienced a moment of pareidolia, seeing several faces in the patterns of decay and laughing to himself that the house must have many secrets to tell. He shrugged it off and wondered if seeing a hippy-type person in the middle of nowhere had prompted him to have an acid flashback. He had often heard the old schoolers speak about their flashbacks from taking LSD but he had never experienced one himself up to that point. Hank blinked his eyes a few times and found himself to be just fine. A fleeting moment of strangeness that he quickly forgot about.

As he got to the bottom of the stairs Bernie pointed at the front door. "They don't make 'em like that anymore," she said in her deep country drawl. The door was eight feet high and looked to be solid oak. It was as old as the rest of the house (Hank and Amy both noticed the cornerstone stating it was built in 1893 on the way to the front door) and had a large oval-shaped piece of rounded glass for its window. It evoked an earlier time, when everything was handmade and folks took a certain pride in their work. Although the porch itself was empty, other than a few antique rocking chairs, it extended across the entirety of the front of the house and continued along the eastern side. The door with its oval window complimented it quite well, tying everything together and giving the place a sense of grandeur both fading and lasting.

"Plenty of room for rocking chairs," Bernice, picking up on what they were both thinking, stated the obvious.

"Just what I was thinking," Amy returned in her neutral southern Illinois accent. "We'll have to put a grill out here Hank. What an awesome porch."

"Yeah, I like that idea a lot. But let's see...you know, we haven't signed a lease yet. Who knows how we'll like the inside, or if it will be right for us," Hank returned casually, but she could tell he was already sold on the place.

"How could he not be?" she thought to herself.

It was perfect. Secluded, relaxing, stress-free country life was what they both needed after their ordeal in Lexington. A simple place to work out of and to grow their marijuana in peace and quiet. She shuddered at the thought of guns in her face, yelling, blue and red lights and those cold cuffs on her wrists. She shuddered again remembering the deal they made for their freedom, the deal that allowed them to be looking for a new life. Before the ramifications of what they had done weighed on her like a bag of bricks on her chest, Amy cleared her throat. "Shall we then?", she motioned towards the door.

"Yeah, go ahead it's unlocked. Take as much time as you need to look around. Just don't go upstairs until I get back. I need to run over to my house for a few minutes. I just stopped by on the way back from town…and shoot, I was already late by then…." Bernice stammered on. "Mom and dad need help this time of day. Couple hours before the sun goes down they have a lot of medicine to take. Let me go take care of that and I will be right back. Probably 15 to 20 minutes tops."

"Ok, great," Hank exclaimed, boyishly excited.

He turned the doorknob as Bernie walked back to her truck and entered a large foyer with high vaulted ceilings and a giant mirror opposite the front door. The wallpaper was old. So old it may have actually been original. There were doors off either side with a hallway continuing around to the right and couches along the walls covered in dust covers so filthy they both wondered as to how anything could be clean underneath. The house had the grime of ages past that was for sure, but it had a unique charm, unlike anything either of them had ever known. Immediately they both felt at home.

They toured the house slowly, but not together. Hank took the left door, and Amy walked right, down the hallway toward what appeared to be the bedrooms. They both found the high ceilings made the place seem much more open than it already was, but the house was filled with more furniture, everywhere they went. Even the kitchen had lots of old furniture and odds and ends. Still, they quite easily imagined where their own possessions would fit. As Hank rounded through the living room and the adjacent den he came through the kitchen and saw Amy standing there with her jaw agape. She looked almost in shock; like something was wrong. He wondered if she had seen a ghost. He approached her cautiously as she seemed to be staring off into space. He reached out to touch her shoulder and just as his hand reached her she began to sob.

"Hank, it is so perfect. So abso-fuckin'-lutely perfect. I can't wait to see the basement, the downstairs, the bedrooms…all of it. But, while she's out, let's go out back and smoke a fat bowl," Amy said with love in her voice as she wiped salty tears off of her cheeks. He thought nothing of her spacing out after she seemed to return to normal cognition. Amy did everything she could to seem normal, but something just wasn't right. She felt faint and nauseous at once, but it subsided after a few deep breathes. She held Hank close and found solace in his embrace, not letting go until she was sure that dizziness had left her.

They went out the back door onto a back porch which was much smaller than the front. It was a typical mid-twentieth century porch completely at odds with the rest of the house. As they made their way into the backyard it was apparent there were several other structures on the property. Two small shacks about fifty yards behind the house were angled forty-five degrees to the rest of the property. They appeared much older than the house and harkened back to frontier times. Dilapidated and pathetic looking, they were quite an eyesore and stood apart from the house itself but shared something in common with the architecture of the town of Gravel Switch. They were truly old edifices and immediately the couple were both stricken with overwhelming curiosity. Hank pulled a glass pipe out of his pocket and Amy got a nugget of fine OG Kush (his favorite strain of marijuana) out of her purse and handed it to him. As he packed the bowl and lit it they began walking across the yard toward the buildings. Neither of the structures still had a door. Both had a single window and were otherwise totally empty. The walls were overgrown with weeds and vines on the inside but were mostly clear outside, as if they had been recently cleaned. The broken pieces of an ancient, rotting stool sat outside the front door of the shack furthest from the house. Nothing special, nothing important, yet even without speaking the two knew that these were indeed very cool buildings, full of history and significance, forgotten relics of a bygone age that had once been the castles of their occupants.

Hank passed the pipe to Amy and exhaled a thick cloud of peppery and sweet fruity smoke. She toked deep off of the bowl and the two began to relax. "Hank, these buildings…you think they were slave quarters?"

"I doubt it, Amy. Slavery was done by the end of the Civil War, but the cornerstone said the house was built in 1893. I bet that those were tool sheds or maybe they hunted and kept their hunting dogs in those shacks. Seems like even for slaves that living in those would be cruel," he spread his arms and used his span to measure the building. "I bet it is only seven feet by ten feet," he was deliberately condescending to try to make her feel ignorant. It worked. He could tell by her body language. Being a dick came to Hank naturally and she knew he didn't mean anything by it, that it was his main character flaw. She tried to let it roll off of her, but his cruelty did affect her sometimes. She buried it and regained composure immediately.

"I bet it would depend on how well they treated their slaves Hank," she returned in a shitty tone and stuck out her tongue to let him know he did it again. He had treated her like an ass for nothing. Hank shook his head in acknowledgment. She handed him back the pipe. He hit it twice before giving it back to her without any green left on top. She shrugged and they walked together over to the garage that was alongside the house and opposite the driveway. The garage was a modern structure made of cinder blocks with a plain door and a padlock on it. It looked to be fifteen feet by twenty feet and Hank immediately knew that if it came with the property rental then it was going to be his glass shop. He would set up his kilns and his torches in there. It was even more perfect for a glass shop than the house was for a grow house. This just kept getting better. Amy was thinking the same thing, he was sure. It couldn't get any more perfect. Just the thought of setting his shop back up got him excited.

As the two were soaking in their new surroundings and basking in the realization that they had found the place of their dreams Bernie showed back up, kicking up dirt and dust, in her rust brown Ford truck. As she parked next to the garage Hank fell to the ground violently, spasming and shaking. His hands contorted into claws of pure tension. Amy rushed to his side and motioned to Bernice in such a way as to let her know this wasn't anything unusual. Amy held his hand for a few moments, until he regained normal composure as Bernice stared off over the fields, trying not to seem like she had seen Hank in such a compromised state.

"Well I guess now is as good a time as any to get this out of the way, but...I have epilepsy and suffer from grand mal seizures," Hank said in such a way that let her know he was alright and clear-headed. "I hope that isn't a problem for you. It is why we want to move out here to the country. It is a lot less stressful and much more relaxing out here and that is really good for my health. I guess I was just stressing on if we were gonna get it and if we were gonna be able to afford it."

"Well you ain't got nothin' to worry about Hank," Bernice said back with a sly smile. "Mom and dad were just tickled pink at the thought of renting this old place out to a couple of young newlyweds in love."

Amy chimed in awkwardly, killing the mood Hank and Bernice had established. "How much is it? That's my biggest worry. A place this big, I know it's old, but…"

"Three hundred a month," Bernie said coolly as if it was non-negotiable and she knew she was asking too much.

"Seriously? Three hundred? Our cable bill was almost that much last month in Lexington," Amy said the words and realized that she had spoken too quickly. The old man they had talked to when they had called did not lie.

"It's a different economy out here. God knows I couldn't've done shit on three hundred bucks when I was in college. But out here…I don't know. Life is slower, everyone is more relaxed and it is pretty much just like it used to be when we were kids. A buck goes a lot farther than it does in the city. Plus mom and dad are just glad to rent the place…they know it ain't in the best shape. It's sat empty for about twenty years now. Only reason we ain't tore it down and planted crops over it is the history of the place and how long it's been in the family. Now, in winter it will cost you more than that to keep it warm, so don't think it's gonna be super affordable all year. With those huge Victorian windows the cold comes right through and winters out here…well, you know. Y'all are from Lexington. "

They had become nearly exhausted just listening to her speak, were totally enamored and were both smiling ear to ear. As Bernice noticed how in her grasp they were she reached into the pocket of her Levi's and pulled out what appeared to Hank and Amy to be at least an eighth ounce of marijuana and a pack of rolling papers. She casually started rolling a joint, which took her all of thirty seconds, and lit it. She took a deep drag off of it and passed it to Hank.

"How did you know we smoke?" Hank asked her with a juvenile innocence in his voice.

"My god, Hank, I could smell y'all as soon as I got out of the truck. I'm no spring chick and you might not know it from looking at me but I used to be a Deadhead. I did several tours, following Jerry and the boys around the country. The Grateful Dead was my life when I was in college. In fact, I even know who you are. I sold you a sheet of LSD in Miami, right before the cops came in and tear-gassed us all," she laughed as she recalled her Deadhead days and the moment she had met Hank nearly fifteen years prior.

"Oh…my…god…" Hank's jaw dropped so hard Amy thought that it would hit the floor. "Amy this is the woman I was telling you about. The one who sold me the best acid I ever got in my life and gave me a ride to the next show after I had been tear gassed and Tony and Laina left me. Oh…my…god!" Hank gushed. He was always excited when random hippies from his past came back into his life. So many years after that scene ended the people of the Grateful Dead community were still who he considered family. At the same time, he knew that Amy would never understand. She had never been there, had never seen the magic of the shows, the people. She had come along in the wake of the Dead. In the era of Phish and the post-Jerry Garcia jam band scene that had become such a blight on the hippie community in Hank's eyes. Amy herself had three boyfriends who had died from various drug overdoses or drugs interacting badly with other drugs. All opiates and amphetamines. He had always secretly felt as if he had saved Amy from the hideous degradation of the hippie scene and showed her an older, kinder way; where the community took care of each other and considered everyone in it to be family. He had neglected to tell her of his teens and early twenties as a street punk. Into hardcore and crust, he had been a gutter punk squatter, a train hopper and a general hobo and scumbag. The sort of people Amy regularly let him know she despised. Yet he had been that very thing for years until he found the Dead family. Once the wolf put on the tie-dyed sheep's clothing he never took it off, yet occasionally he thought back to those days of hard living and hard drugs. Of living on the edge of death. Stealing and robbing, sleeping in laundromats and ditches. Fucking random girls whose names eluded him. He had a deep past that she knew little about and he intended to keep it that way. For all she knew he had always been a successful weed grower, one of the few kids in Lexington with the force of will strong enough to make his own path.

Bernice and Amy were both just staring at Hank, giving him silly looks, trying to get his attention. He finally noticed and realized that he had been spacing out, thinking weird thoughts that had begun to ramble through the back of his mind and into the forefront of consciousness. Hank realized he had never passed the joint and more than a few seconds had passed. He gave the doobie over to Amy and laughed at himself.

The rest of the evening they sat on the porch drinking beer from Bernice's cooler and matching her joint for joint. After smoking for a few hours they paid her their first month's rent and another three hundred dollars as a security deposit. She gave them both a copy of the key and explained where their yard ended and the fields began. As she was getting in her truck to leave she turned and threw another key on a separate ring over to Hank with a strong overhand toss. He missed the key and laughed as it slid across the porch.

"What's that one for?" he asked.

"The garage. You get the garage too. And both the slave quarters, but I doubt you'll need those. Nobody's used them in at least eighty years. My great-grandmother had a tenant who used to kennel his dogs in them in the winter, but they're kinda overgrown now," she laughed to herself a little as she saw the looks on their faces.

"We were wondering what those buildings were," Hank said. "But the cornerstone says the house was built in eighteen ninety-three. That's twenty-eight years after the Civil War ended."

"Yeah, the place was burnt to the ground by the damn Yankees during the war. It was rebuilt in eighteen ninety-three," she said matter of factly as if delivering a history lesson to students. "Sorry. Accidentally put my history professor hat on. I used to teach American history at UK."

She turned back towards her truck and opened the door to get in. Realizing she had one last agenda to address before retiring home she turned back to them and said, "Oh, one last thing. Don't go upstairs until I come back by tomorrow to clean it out. It's gonna take us a few weeks to clean everything out. You saw all the old furniture, so you know how much there is. We'll keep your rent, you can stay through that time, but we won't officially start charging you 'til next month. I'll be by tomorrow to start loading stuff up. I'll get the power turned on for you tomorrow too. Tonight you'll have to use candles if you choose to stay. Alright y'all, have a good night."

With that she got in her truck, waved goodbye and backed down the driveway. Hank and Amy opened the trunk of their car and got out an air mattress. They set it up in the living room and lit a few tea candles for light. They made love for hours and held each other after, talking of all their hopes and dreams for the future.

In the middle of the night, Hank woke suddenly, sitting bolt upright with a start. He found he was sweating profusely and his heart was racing. The sound of a large thud upstairs had jolted him right out of his deep and pleasant dreams. He shook Amy until she awoke, annoyed, and demanded he go back to sleep.

"It's an old house, Hank. They make noise, they settle. It's nothing. It may be an animal in the attic. Bernie will take care of it tomorrow."

With that she exhaled loudly through her nostrils and rolled over. Her annoyed state was obvious, yet it left Hank confused. She was the superstitious one out of the two of them. As he rolled over on his side to hold her, he peered out the window and caught a glimpse of something bright red in the field that was his new front yard. He got out of bed, put his pants on and walked out the front door. He lit a cigarette and stood on the porch, looking around casually for the red blur he had seen. Was it a light? A Passing car, way out on the road? Maybe he was just high? As all of those thoughts were stricken down by his powers of deduction he looked out from the side of the porch, around the north side of the house, and saw for the first time that he had a large black barn adjacent to his yard. He didn't wonder how he failed to notice it when he first walked around the yard earlier that afternoon. He just stared. He drew deep off of his cigarette and stared at the barn. In the moon-light the dark planks that made it up shone a ghastly grey like very old black paint. The barn door was open and the portal stood out as much darker than the rest of the barn. A perfect square of pure black. He could feel something staring back at him. He fixated on the barn door and drew deeply off of his cigarette. As he exhaled a thick cloud of smoke he saw two red lights appear in the barn door. "Were they lights?" he thought. "No. They were reflecting the moon. Whatever they are they aren't lights." He took a step to the right and the two red things moved with him. He took a step back and then a step to the left and they moved with him again. He began to feel the hair on the back of his neck stand up. The air smelled strangely of ozone, like right before a thunderstorm. He closed his eyes slowly in a deep blink before deciding to go investigate but as he opened his eyes back up realized that the two red things he was perceiving were themselves eyes as they had blinked back at him. He felt cold and nauseous all at once and knew immedi-ately that he was in danger of some unknown, eldritch sort the likes of which he had never imagined. He wondered if he was going crazy. Surely he was. Yet no danger had ever felt so imminent.

In a panic he took an immediate step back, turned on his heel abruptly and ran the length of the porch back to the front door. He opened it in a frenzy and slammed it. When he got back to the living room where they had put out their air mattress he was shocked to find Amy fast asleep and undis-turbed by his slamming of the door. He crawled into bed with her and put his arm around her. He held her close and kissed her neck.

"I love you, Amy. But I think I'm going crazy," he admitted as he lay awake, too afraid to close his eyes.

THE ATTIC AND THE DOLL

$\mathcal{T}$he days that followed were without much incident; mellow and calm for Amy and relaxing for Hank, save a few seizures. Bernice did not show up to clean out any of the furniture for a solid week, which they would soon come to understand was standard for country folk. A day was a week. A week a month. Everyone seemed to operate on a slower schedule than they said they would. The Hickmans had their farmhands around the property often, but they themselves remained unseen by Hank and Amy other than Bernice.

The day she did show up she came with a crew of men and several vehicles. A flatbed truck among them. They intended to take everything. Several couches, love seats, armoires, chests of drawers, a few beds and tables. Lamps, chandeliers, mirrors and all sorts of odds and ends. Trunks, chests, and cabinets were going as well as all of the contents of the as yet unexplored and enigmatic attic. As the crew began to haul off the largest items Amy was haggling with Bernice about keeping a few things. She got the large mirror in the foyer, a nice oak four-poster bed, an armoire, a silver tea service that looked like it was from the eighteenth century. She got several chests and trunks as well as some gardening tools from rakes and shovels to a wheelbarrow and even a lawnmower. Bernice told her to keep everything but Amy insisted she pay at least something, so they compromised with the decision that they would use the lawnmower to keep the three and a half acres of yard mowed for the first year of their occupancy. Amy agreed without talking to Hank and shrugged it off. She considered that if he didn't want to do it then she could always do it herself. It would give her a bit of a chance to have some time to herself anyway. Just put on some headphones, crank up the music and space out while mowing. She actually looked forward to it. Lastly, Bernice informed her that the upstairs was cleared out, except for one room which was full of antiques which had all belonged to the former tenants over the years.

"You feel free to use the room, but please leave everything up there where it's at," Bernie said. "Some of that stuff is over a hundred years old, believe it or not. And mom 'n dad want it to stay up there, but there's also plenty of room. Honestly, I'd probably grow myself a crop up there if I was ya'll," she concluded jovially. Amy shot her a sly smile and winked. It was perfect. The landlord had no problems with what they intended to use the house for. It was a one in a million payoff, or so it seemed to Amy in that moment.

The day after the big move Hank had three of his friends from Lexington come down to help him move his own things into the house. They brought a U-Haul filled with all of Hank's stuff from his storage shed in Lexington. Amy's mother came out the following day with another U-Haul. Within another day they were nearly set up, feeling in their own place, feeling at home.

As the weeks went by Hank set up his glass shop in the garage and began making glass pipes, paperweights, marbles and beads. He went into the upstairs one day to see what he could do as far as setting up a grow operation. There was the main room, which was essentially the master bedroom of the house. Off to the left, as he came up the tower stairs, was another large room which in turn had another room off of it. That was where he intended to put his grow. He set up his hydroponic tables over an afternoon and soon was on his way to producing a high-quality crop of indoor cannabis. After setting up his grow tables he decided to explore the attic. There was another door off of the right side of the master bedroom and it was the only place left that the attic could be; the attic he had worked himself up so much about.

He took a deep breath and stole himself against his anxiety. An anxiety that he realized was both overwhelming and irrational. Hank noticed that his palms were sweating and his brow was furrowed. He had become tense and was hunching a bit, he could tell. He turned the knob, half expecting to walk into a nightmare from one of his shock horror films; the ones Amy loathed so much but was kind enough to watch with him. Instead, he was met with a plain, empty stairway, dusty and moldy smelling. It was well lit by a skylight that he had failed to notice when looking at the roof from the road and the yard. He ascended the stairs and rounded a waist-high rail at the top and found a room full of mostly shelving, a few trunks and chests which were highly dust-covered, and not much else. Not much at all for how much space there was, but what was there was quite odd and he made a note of it as he remembered Bernie telling him that they were all belongings of the previous tenants. There was an old oil lamp, a compound bow, a square cardboard box that had German writing on it and an image of a black eagle clutching a swastika. Hank was astounded. There was also a world war two U.S. Army officer's long coat, a tie-dyed tapestry hung on the wall and lastly in the corner there was a chair covered with a dust cloth. Hank got an uneasy feeling as he observed that the chair didn't have feet sticking out from under the cloth but wheels. It was an antique wheel-chair and he had the feeling right away that it had been used at an asylum. For when he began to peel back the thickly caked dust cloth, that he could neither identify as gray nor brown, he saw deep gouges in the wood of the arm rests, which had bind-ings on them for securing the patient. He gulped in shock as if seeing the moment of a struggle to free himself from that very chair. The thing of his nightmares made real before him. Hank imagined a frail skeleton underneath the shroud as he slowly pulled on it. He thought that he had never been more creeped out in his life, but he thought this too soon. Hank pulled the dust cloth fully off of the chair, kicking up a thick cloud of noxious, antique dust. "The very curse of the mummy's tomb," he thought and after the cloud settled he was met with the blood-chilling visage of a doll so foul he almost vomited at the sight of it.

What pleasure or delight any child had ever gotten from the wretched thing Hank could not imagine. It looked as if more than a century of neglect had taken its toll on the doll, then it was buried under shit and walked through hell back to the mortal and physical restrictions of our regular everyday reality. It was something from a nightmare yet Hank could not tear his eyes away. Patches of straw-like hair barely clung to the charred-looking scalp, whose paint had all but worn off. If the head had once been porcelain or wood, Hank could not even say. The doll was caked with grime and filth some of which he thought might be blood or feces stains. It was missing the right arm and the left was half covered in tattered, rotting fabric. The dress was missing, except for other tattered shreds and Hank could not identify the cloth's material it was so dilapidated. The body appeared to be stuffed with straw, which was falling out of it in clumps. The lips were brownish black and seemed as though they had once been painted a nice crimson. The nose was missing, somehow Hank's perception was that it had been somewhere between smashed and gnawed off. But it was the eyes he could not peel his gaze from. They seemed as though they had once been beautiful enamels yet they had no shine, nor sparkle to them. Whatever had been inlayed in them had fallen out. Hank assumed glass for the pupils and irises and ivory for the whites, yet all that remained were two black pits, peeling at whatever wretched and abominable material she was constructed of.

*H*ank awoke on the floor just as he usually did when recovering from a seizure when alone. He could see that he had covered the doll back up with the cloth as it was back in place on the wheelchair. Good. He didn't want to see that thing again. He knew she would definitely be giving him nightmares tonight. He tried to drive the image of her out of his head, yet could not do it. "How old is she?" he wondered. Older than the house he was sure of that, but just how old?

He gathered his composure and went back downstairs. He staggered into the kitchen and fumbled to a cabinet where he kept his medications. He took a Valium and his seizure medication and went into the living room where he found Amy napping on the couch. He packed a bud of his signature marijuana into the bowl of his favorite pipe and began to mellow out a bit after inhaling deeply, holding the smoke until he coughed. He shook Amy until she awoke groggily.

"I have something I really need you to see. Seriously Amy. Go upstairs, up through the door on the right, into the attic. Go look at what is under the cloth on the chair. Seriously, just go… look. Tell me I'm not crazy Amy. Oh, yeah. I had a seizure while I was up there. Don't know how long I was out," he tried to convey a sense of urgency with his words that she was simply not responsive to.

Amy rubbed her eyes as she replied, "Fuck you, Hank. You wake me up for this shit. I'll go, but this is bullshit. I did need to wake up though. But you know you'd be pissed if I did that to you, sweetie." She winked at him to let him know she was joking with him, at least halfway.

"I know. That's why I'm being so serious. This is some crazy shit. You just have to see it for yourself. Take a picture or two while you are up there. Plus I got the hydro tables set up while you were napping," he said with self-pride.

He handed her his pipe to take with her and her digital camera to take pictures with. She took a deep toke off of the pipe and headed to the back of the house, toward the stairs. A couple of minutes later and Hank heard a loud thud, followed by Amy's high pitched scream. She came tearing down the stairs a few moments later. Waving her camera frantically at Hank.

"Baby, you gotta see this! That fuckin' thing is alive or something," she was shaking and could barely get the words out. Her skin had gone pale and she seemed dizzy and trying to steady herself by waving her camera at Hank. She walked over to him and showed him the display screen. He felt a sense of panic and shock at what he saw. It made the doll a thousand times creepier to him. It appeared exactly the same except where the hollow black pits it had for eyes had been there was a blue, fiery glow. Emanating from that foul thing some strange and unnamable energy was casting its blue light throughout the picture. She showed him eight such pictures just the same. Every one with glowing blue eyes.

"I want that thing out of this house immediately!" she demanded.

"I do too baby," Hank said as he headed back upstairs to get the doll.

He returned a moment later with the doll, gripping it about the waist forcefully in order to keep all of its stuffing inside where he felt it belonged. Hank walked to the front door and put the doll on top of a heap of rubbish and odds and ends that he was throwing out with the garbage.

That night neither of them could sleep. They both lay in bed, playing o'possum and trying not to disturb the other. Just after they had gotten up and eaten breakfast they heard a loud knock at the front door.Hank answered to find Bernice standing there with her back to the door, gasping in joy. She turned slowly as if she didn't put it together that he had actually answered the door at first and was embarrassed by it. When she met his gaze he saw that she was holding the doll close to her chest and cradling it like a young girl with her favorite dolly.

"You found my doll Hank!" she exclaimed with more enthusiasm than he had ever in his life seen from a woman in her thirties. "It's been missing for 'bout twenty years...my god! You found her. Matilda is her name. She was my three times great granny's doll. Made during the civil war by hand, right here in Marion County."

He was flabbergasted at how fast she spoke. It was obvious that she was very passionate about the doll. As she talked on and on about how "gorgeous Matilda was and still is," Hank realized he had not even yet spoken a word.

He interrupted her, but not rudely, to ask, "would you like to come in for some coffee and smoke a joint before I get working today Bernie?"

"No. Thanks though," she shook her head. "I gotta be gettin' back to mom 'n dad, just dropped by to get Matilda. I heard you'd found her and was just tickled to death. See you later Hank, tell Amy I said hi." And with that, she turned on her heel, walked down the porch steps, across the yard and got in her truck. He went inside as she backed down the driveway, blaring Willy Nelson's Still is Still Movin' on her stereo too loud for such an early hour, even out in the middle of nowhere.

As Hank recounted the events to Amy over morning coffee they both had to wonder just how it was that Bernie had heard they found her doll. Why she would even want such a creepy, rotting, old piece of history had as a question, for the most part, fallen to the wayside of the road of their collective thinking. They both let their paranoia get the best of them and Hank began to suffer from anxiety. Eventually, he had a severe seizure and was unable to get any work done that day. He felt weak all day and took two long naps on the couch. When he awoke from the second nap he found Amy was gone and had taken their car. She had left a bowl packed in their pipe in front of him on the coffee table and he lit it and smoked until he was truly stoned. Then and only then did he bother to read the note she left him.

*H*ank,
     I went to get some answers about that crazy fucking doll.

Somebody around here knows something.
I think I know where to start looking.
There's some KFC chicken in the fridge
I might be home late, but will let you know as
Soon as I know something.
Love,
Amy
"Well fuck," he said to no one but himself.

3

THE HISTORIAN AND THE PLEA

*a*my drove through the morning fog with a grim determination to get to the bottom of things. She was used to weirdness, for sure, being a hippie and having taken her fair share of psychedelic drugs. Their first night in Gravel Switch she had taken two tabs of MDMA, as had Hank, though she had not been high like that since. What was going on in her home, with her landlord and with that god-forsaken doll she could not say. However a month ago she had met a queer old woman at the Sunday farmer's market. She was strange and worldly beyond even the most eccentric folks in the area. Phyllis was her name. Phyllis Jenkins the county historian.

"Or she used to be..." Amy said out loud as she rounded a tight corner and lit a cigarette. Her blonde hair was dirty and greasy from not showering. She slept very little the night before. Something in the energy of that doll. She just couldn't shake it. Whatever the phenomenon was she captured on film it was unwanted and unwelcome. Where she came from dolls did not have glowing blue eyes. Nor did they rot for a hundred years in some forgotten attic, sitting like a little person in a creepy old wheelchair. She knew she was being unreasonable to be so freaked out by a doll, but she also knew there was no way in hell Bernie could have known they found her in the attic. Matilda. The thing had a name. Yeah, that was creepy too.

Amy arrived just after eight o'clock that morning at the address Phyllis had provided. It was less than five miles from Amy's house as the crow flies, but it was a fifteen-minute drive for Amy who did not know the extremely curvy roads. She drove down the very short driveway of a decrepit old surf green trailer that had not seen good days since the nineteen seventies. There were several chickens in the yard and a goat with black and white spots chewing hay in a pen beside the trailer. Phyllis had no vehicle of her own on the property but Amy could see the front door was open. "I hope she's home. Maybe she doesn't have a car," Amy thought out loud.

As soon as she turned off the ignition and opened her door to get out of the car Phyllis appeared in the doorway and stepped out onto the front porch. Her hair was in curlers and she was wearing a beat up old maroon nightgown that appeared to have once been quite expensive, but much like the trailer, had seen better days. She had a coffee mug in her hand and didn't seem to notice, or perhaps she just didn't mind, when she spilled some coffee on one of her pink bunny slippers.

"Welcome, Amy. Good to see ya again sugar," Phyllis said with the kind smile that only a woman over seventy could give. Motherly and wise, tender and nurturing all at once. Amy immediately felt a draw to Phyllis. In fact, she felt as drawn to Phyllis as she felt repulsed by Matilda. She admitted to herself that she was indeed a bit uneasy about that aspect of her arrival.

"Good to see you, Phyllis. Thanks for having me over. I

really appreciate it, especially so early and on such short notice. You won't believe what happened...I mean, I don't believe what happened and I am a bit scared," Amy immediately began to stammer, as if she had too much to say and was afraid of missing any single minute detail of the situation.

"Let's get you inside dear. How do you take your coffee?" Phyllis asked, continuing to be nurturing, which calmed Amy down a bit.

As Amy entered the trailer it was not anything at all like she thought it would be on the inside. She had assumed that it would be filled with hundreds of ceramic figures, the kind that were ubiquitous in the homes of elderly single ladies. Instead, she found sparse furnishings and paintings everywhere; paintings that Phyllis had obviously done herself and they were quite psychedelic. Splashes of color washing across strange angles describing otherworldly, non-euclidian architecture on some paintings. Occult themes and arcane symbols dominated other paintings. Wards against the unholy...or were they intended to summon something? Amy could not tell, but she knew that Phyllis was on an entirely different level than herself. There were strange herbs tied in bundles and drying all through the living room, hanging from the ceiling and giving the house a strong, unfamiliar smell. As Amy curiously sniffed the air she felt Phyllis's eyes on her.

"Wolf's bane," the old woman stated plainly, leaving Amy wondering if Phyllis could somehow read her mind.

"I was wondering what that was," Amy admitted, sheepishly.

"Sit dear. We obviously have much to discuss," Phyllis gestured for Amy to take a seat around her dining room table. The only table that Amy could actually see in the trailer. It was empty other than a large, black, leather-bound book. It seemed to be as old as Matilda. A relic from a bygone age. Amy knew that much of what she wanted to know may be included in that tome. As she settled into her seat Phyllis put a hot cup of coffee in front of her.

"It has half 'n half and two spoons of sugar, just like you take it dear."

"Wow…uh, thanks. But, how did you know how I take my coffee? We've only just met," Amy said before she took a long, much-needed sip off of the cup.

"I'm psychic dear. I just know things. It's part of my gift. Been runnin' in my family for as long as we know of…well, the women folk at least. All the way back to my four times great granny. I don't know if you believe in that sorta thing, but that's all I know," Phyllis laid it all out. "Now what has happened that's got you all shook up?"

"We moved into town a few months back. Me and my husband Hank. He has bad seizures, so we wanted to move out to the country and be in peace. We found a place that hadn't been rented for twenty years and have been living there…"

"You moved into the Hickman place. The old farmhouse, not the new place…no, their daughter Bernice would be living there then," Phyllis muttered in a low voice. "I had hoped this wasn't the case."

"Yes. Exactly. The Hickman place. Before you tell me what is going on with it let me finish. It's weird," Amy said. The city girl in her was not offended by being interrupted. Yet somehow she was offended, just a bit, so realized that the country was already rubbing off on her.

"Go on dear," Phyllis let Amy continue.

"We have had a few weird things happen. I keep hearing voices, but when nobody else is home. Some are women, some are men. Some are children though and it's getting really frightening. The longer I live there the more often I hear them and the clearer they get. I used to not be able to tell what they were saying but now it's as plain as day. God…I haven't even told Hank about that part. Geez….maybe I should, but then we found this doll in the attic. I mean it is fucking weird. Like at least a hundred years old and pretty much rotting to pieces. The thing is I took pictures of it and in the pictures, a blue light was pouring out of the eyes," Amy said as she pulled her digital camera out of her purse and showed the pictures to Phyllis who just nodded. Not in disbelief, but as if the images were reaffirming what she already knew.

"Amy dear, you are in grave danger."

"I sorta get that feeling Phyllis, that's why I'm here. I want to know what to do. Oh, yeah…I almost forgot. Bernice came by the morning after we found the doll. We had thrown it in a rubbish heap on the front porch. Mostly debris from around the house that we couldn't fit in the trash can this week. She knocked on the door all excited and told Hank she was so happy we found her dolly, said it was named Matilda. We have no idea at all how she knew. We didn't even talk to anybody. I'm freaking out over it. She was so weird about it," Amy exclaimed, almost in a panic. She was obviously afraid and feeling anxiety.

"Matilda. Yes, that would make sense," Phyllis muttered half to herself. "Amy my dear, that house is a wound on the very fabric of creation. Sure, that weird old doll is scary I'm sure. As well as some of the other things I've heard were in that attic. But the house itself, it is evil. You couldn't pay me a million dollars to set foot in it, even for a minute.

"The legends surrounding it are many and the truth can often be hard to distinguish from fiction. But rest assured, that house feeds on its residents. It is a vile plague on this community, hell, on this earth itself. My granny used to say it was the place where the devil landed when he fell to earth. Now I don't know if that is true, but it is irrelevant because for all intents and purposes it acts as such. Now it may not even be the house itself either, so much as the land it is on, which also has its own twisted history."

Amy stared on, nodding and absorbing everything Phyllis said as if her life depended on it. She breathed in deeply. When Phyllis paused to let her speak or ask questions Amy remained silent and waited for the old woman to continue, hanging on every word.

"In the seventeen hundreds, French fur trappers were making their way through this part of Kentucky when they came upon a group of Indians. Pawnee who had come across the Ohio River to hunt before the winter. The story goes that the French approached peacefully and traded with the Pawnee that day. Everything was fine until the next day when the braves were out hunting. The fur trappers came back to the Indian camp. They massacred everyone there. All women and children. They took all of their scalps and all of their furs and food. It is said that the braves returned to find the French taking turns raping the last living girl and a fierce fight broke out. Only one brave survived. They say he cursed the land. He called for a scourge to forever come to eat his enemies.

"Sixty years later the Hickman family built the first house on that very spot. The spot where your house is now. They were the ones used to run everything around here. Back in the early eighteen hundreds, they were the richest family around. But, as you know we had a big battle right here during the war between the states. Perryville. Truth be told neither side won. The Yankees lost many times more men, but the Confederacy was forced out of Kentucky permanently. But I digress…"

Amy sat transfixed. She looked Phyllis right in the eye for all of it. For a moment she pondered just how beautiful the old woman's blue-green eyes were and noted just how pretty she must have been in her day, though there were no pictures around to verify this notion.

Phyllis stood up, went into the kitchen with both of their mugs and topped off both of their coffees. She returned to the dining room, sat both cups on the table and went immediately back into the kitchen. A silver platter like the one from the antique tea service Amy found in her attic was in Phyllis's hands. On the tray were several colas of high-grade marijuana, some rolling papers, an ashtray and a lighter. "Roll one up for us dear, my arthritis is acting up, I can't roll too good right now," Phyllis said before continuing the story. Amy wasn't shocked at all that the old psychic used marijuana medically to help her arthritis. She nodded in agreement and began to roll a joint.

"Now after the fighting at Perryville men from both sides were lost. Scattered, running for their lives through the thick of these woods and hills right here in Gravel Switch. As it so happened a group of about ten to twelve Confederate soldiers found the Hickman house, which at the time was occupied by the youngest of the Hickman sons, his wife and kids and their two slaves, Sheridan and Matilda. They took everyone hostage and used the house to hole up in until the Yankee patrols stopped scouring the area. Well everyone that is except Matilda who was out in the fields when they showed up, walking home from a farm down the road, warning the neighbors the fighting was getting close to home. She, seeing the rebels take her husband and her master's family hostage, ran as fast as she could away from the house. She ran straight into a group of U.S. Army cavalrymen who were hunting for the very rebels she was fleeing. She told them everything, begged for them to save her family. Told them right were to go and they did. But when they got there they met stiff resistance. Tired of losing men the Lieutenant ordered the house be burned to the ground with everyone in it. They set it ablaze and rode on. Everyone inside burned to a crisp, all down in that basement," as Phyllis spoke a strange darkness fell over her face.

"Oh my god," was all Amy could say as she toked on the fat joint that she had rolled from Phyllis' tray. She passed it to Phyllis without saying a word, desperately wanting to hear more. So intrigued by the story she had forgotten where it was going, or even that it pertained to her and her own strange situation.

"Nobody knows what happened to Matilda. That is why I am finding it, well a bit funny, that she said the doll's name was Matilda. I guess the Hickman's loved her to death though. Matilda's daughter was owned by the head of the family, the father of the one who burned with the house. After the fire they set her free out of pity after she lost her dad, and her mother went missing. She continued to live on the Hickman farm and eventually married one of them. They had a child and that is who all the Hickmans in this area today are descended from, as the rest of the family line fell ill with consumption."

"Consumption?" Amy asked curiously.

"That's what they used to call tuberculosis," Phyllis informed her before continuing. "Amy that house you live in today is built right on top of the site of that fire, right on the same foundation. The spirits there are unrestful. The Hickmans have known since the turn of the century that the house was home to more than just the people who lived there. It is still home to all the people who died there…but also to something else. Something ancient. Something unfathomable by the human mind, imperceivable in its entirety by our limited senses and our shallow understanding. Amy, it is the very home of a wickedness that was old itself before the earth even formed in the wake of the sun. It feeds on fear, death, paranoia. It drives the weak minded mad and the strong-willed to the breaking point.

"You are not the first to willingly walk into its grasp. Nor will you be the last. It almost had me once myself. It took the man I love from me….and that's all I'm going to say about it. I just don't want it to happen to you. You are too young and you seem like a nice girl. Anywhere else you could live would be a good idea. But I fear if you stay in that house then it will be the death of you… and it won't be pretty. I don't want to see another life ruined. It's fed enough already!" she began to shake and spill coffee as she deeply hit the joint Amy rolled to try to calm down. Phyllis obviously had an emotional attachment to the house and one of its occupants that was motivating her to convince Amy to leave.

Still, Amy was afraid. Much more so than she had been before the visit, which was saying something. Still, she felt she had pushed Phyllis too far in asking for help on this subject as she watched a tear run down the poor old woman's cheek. Amy got the feeling Phyllis was irrevocably scarred by her own personal experience.

She got up to leave, gave Phyllis a deep hug like one would give an old friend and walked to the front door. She knew there was much more to learn and that Phyllis knew what she herself desperately wanted to know, but Amy also knew she had pushed the old woman too far. She opted to return soon to finish the conversation.

As she stepped out on the front porch Phyllis said, "come back soon dear. We'll finish this tale, you'll see that I'm not puttin' you on about all this. And if you see any of those damn coyotes you be careful. They aren't what they seem. Especially the ones with the red eyes. If you see one of them, well…you come tell me okay." Phyllis followed Amy out to her car to see her off and handed her one of the bundles of wolf's bane. "Take this dear and stay safe."

Amy put the bundle in the passenger's seat and backed out of the driveway. As she began to drive home she noticed that the sun was directly overhead. The clock said noon, yet she felt she had only been inside for an hour. Just long enough to smoke a joint and have a couple of cups of coffee. She drove home without giving it much thought.

When she arrived Hank was on the front porch with his head in his hands. He did not move as she approached. "Hank, what's wrong?" she asked.

He didn't speak, just motioned at the front door. It was covered in writing. Writing that was obviously in blood that said, Ia Shub-Niggurath. There were strange symbols drawn beneath the words. Symbols that Amy had only recently seen at Phyllis's house in her paintings. On the doorstep, atop the welcome mat was perched a severed pig's head. Tongue lolling out to the side. One of the symbols from the door, a spiral shape, drawn on its forehead.

"What the fuck is going on Amy?" Hank asked, choking back tears, his voice cracking like a pubescent boy.

"We're fucked, Hank. That's what's going on. We need to get the hell out of here right now," Amy said with a dire sense of urgency.

"What about our grow Amy? We can't go anywhere for at least a month," Hank reminded her.

Hank sighed deeply and held his wife close.

4

THE DOCTOR

*A*fter several months had passed and summer gave way into a cold fall, Hank and Amy found themselves comfortable, part of the local community and free of any thoughts of the weirdness that had ensued over the spring and summer. Hank had become somewhat of a local celebrity as the only glass blower around. He soon found a thriving local market for his pipes and other wares. Everyone and their mom smoked marijuana in Marion County and soon his glass wares became status symbols among, most especially, the local marijuana growers.

As he built a strong clientele for his glass wares he found a few key individuals who were interested in his strain of hydroponic cannabis. Again he made a name for himself as his product was head and shoulders above and beyond the outdoor, local weed. It wasn't that the strains were poor or that the other growers were unskilled. It was that Hank had a green thumb and attention to detail that few marijuana growers possessed. It wasn't long before Hank had grown considerable clout in the community. With that large farmhouse and huge yard, he would invite his friends from Lexington out in droves to party. They set up makeshift stages, or used the front porch, for his friends' bands to play. They had barbecue and keg parties and all the Lexingtonians were able to mingle with and meet the country folk in a natural and organic way that otherwise would not have occurred.

As Hank enjoyed his new celebrity status Amy found a niche of her own. She started a sewing business and converted one of the spare bedrooms into a sewing room, another spare bedroom into storage for her fabrics. It was still used for guests as a bedroom, but half of it was dominated by stack after stack of Rubbermaid tubs full of fabrics. She took a job managing a Walgreen's pharmacy in Danville, some thirty minutes drive from her home, and settled into her role with a natural ease. She enjoyed the slower pace of country life and found it easy to converse and bond with the people who came into the store.

Jared was one such person she met at work. He was a doctor at the University of Kentucky hospital in Lexington who happened to have grown up in Marion County and lived in Bradfordsville. Amy was immediately attracted to him. He was tall, probably six foot five, and he had thick, curly, shoulder-length hair that bounced slightly as he walked. Dark eyes and a dark complexion he was obviously Melungeon. He always stopped in on his way home from work and got an Ale-8-One, Kentucky's signature soft drink. He would stay and chat with Amy when no one else was in the store or if it was extremely slow. Always in his blue scrubs from the hospital and always more flirtatious than he should be with a married woman. Still, she found herself inviting him over for their next big party.

"Jared, come by my house this weekend. We are having a bonfire party Saturday night, on into Sunday. There's gonna be bands and at least one keg. Lots of people will be there. You'll probably know some of 'em," the words came out of her mouth with much more of a drawl than they would have a couple of months prior. The country was having a quick influence of how she spoke. This time she became acutely aware and got a little embarrassed as she spoke to him. Her cheeks went flushed. She batted her eyes at him in nervousness as he was slow to answer.

"I'd love to come by. Been wanting to get a pipe from your husband anyway," he said in an assuring tone.

More to remind herself than him she said, "his name's Hank."

"Oh, okay," Jared said as he lost his toothy, almost cheesy smile and adopted a look that betrayed a little disappointed that his rival now had a name. "Can't wait to meet him," he lied obviously.

Seeing no one else in the store Amy jotted down her number on an old receipt and handed it to Jared. Letting her fingers graze his, ever so slightly and lingering just a little too long. She came out from behind the counter and lifted her arms up demanding a hug. He met her embrace and was lost in time. Neither of them knew how long they held one another, but both knew it had been far too long to speak about, but not as long as either of them wanted. Jared got a stiff erection almost immediately and became embarrassed. He tried to pull back but Amy put her hand on his lower back and pushed him towards her, surprising both of them. She let out a soft sigh as she felt him throbbing against her. When they let each other go his erection was more than obvious through his scrubs. He turned to walk out the door, his face turning beet red as he noticed an elderly woman had entered the store and was staring at them, needing help getting a pack of cigarettes from behind the counter.

He lifted his hand and waved goodbye awkwardly, walking out of the store so fast he almost ran straight into the automatic door before it could open for him. "See ya Saturday," he said, simply to try to distract both Amy and the old woman from his boner.

"See ya then Jared," Amy blew him a kiss and turned her attention back to the old woman. "What can I get ya, Ethel?"

"I'll take a carton of Misty-Ultra-light-One-Twenty-Menthol-Slims," Ethel rattled off casually.

"Wow, what a mouthful," Amy muttered to herself as she found the carton and rang up the purchase. Turning back to Ethel she said, "that'll be thirty-eight seventy-four sweetheart."

Ethel swiped her credit card and took her carton of cigarettes and her receipt. As she turned to leave she smiled at Amy and breathed in deeply before laying out her truth. "A cock that big only comes along once in a lifetime on a man that good looking. I'd jump right on that if I was you, dear. I see that wedding ring, but whoo whee...um, um, um... fine-lookin' man."

As Ethel walked out to her car Amy knew she had just been hit in the face with the kind of wisdom only one who had lived a long and full life, who knew about love and regrets, could deliver. She stood for some time with her mouth wide open and let the truth of it all sink in.

5

THE PARTY

he next day Hank and Amy threw their big bonfire party and all of the people they had invited came; with the exception of Hank's old friend from childhood, Chris Wilson, who had to work that Saturday night. He was a father of three young children, so Hank forgave him easily enough, though he still kept his fingers crossed in hopes that Chris would come out Sunday for the aftermath. He'd offered to let Chris have the stage to himself to play his bass guitar for the cleanup on Sunday, but still didn't have much faith that he'd see his old friend. Otherwise, Hank was ecstatic. He went about his day with an ear to ear smile and had smoked much more than his usual copious amount of marijuana. After all of the festivities had been properly arranged he knew he had no other responsibilities than to enjoy himself. So Hank dropped seven hits of LSD. It had been a long time since he had tripped on acid and he wanted to have a blast. It came on quite strong after about a half an hour and he wandered around the crowd gathered in his front yard as the first band played and everyone danced. Their music was fun for Hank and apparently the whole crowd. It was a bluegrass-infused heavy metal fusion and the band introduced themselves as the Keepers of the Threshold. As he began to slip away into his psychedelic daydream Hank realized he hadn't seen Amy in over an hour. "She must still be in the house," he thought. "I bet she wants to trip too… I'll go dose her and we'll spin together. No, no. I have to hide from her that I'm trippin'. She'll get mad at me. I could have a seizure…she won't be down." He went back and forth in his head about how he thought she would react.

On the way to his back porch, he ran into Michael and Kelly Williams. A young, married couple from Gravel Switch that Hank had recently befriended. They were kind-hearted and liked to laugh and smoked a lot of weed, so Hank was always happy to hang out with them. His only qualm with them was that they were a bit slow. Much slower than Hank was used to. He had never heard such a thick country drawl as the one that rolled off of Michael's tongue.

"Well hey there, buddy! Great party bro!" Michael exclaimed jovially and his barrel chest roared as he laughed. He had one of those baby faces that looked a bit ridiculous on a man as fat as he was, a solid three-fifty, and Hank tried as hard as he could to hold in a guffaw as Michael spoke.

"Hey, Kelly, Michael! Great to see you," Hank managed to be courteous despite being higher than he had been in over a decade. He realized that sounds were beginning to distort a bit and that words sounded stroboscopic to his ears. "Sorry if I'm weird, I just ate a lot of acid…I'm higher than fuck. Can you help me get to the back door and into the house, I gotta find Amy. Oh, yeah…you wanna eat some acid?" Hank knew from previous conversations with the two that they had never tripped before but that they were curious.

"My god, yeah," they said simultaneously. "We'd love to. Thanks. And sure we'll help you to the house," Michael finished.

"Stick out your tongues."

Hank dropped a tiny, quarter-inch square piece of white paper on both of their tongues. Kelly took Hank by the hand and led him through the yard, around the back, and up the porch. They took him through the back door, through the house and sat him on the couch in the living room. He had forgotten all about finding Amy and closed his eyes for a second to focus on the music. The Keepers of the Threshold were weaving a thick groove of fuzzed out stoner psychedelia with a crazy banjo solo that took Hank to a very calm place. It was mesmerizing in just the right way for how high he was and he immediately felt more comfortable and seemed to have more of his wits about him. He thought about how special this party was and how many different worlds he was able to bring together; the country and the city, the young and the old. He was impressed with himself.

When he opened his eyes he found that Michael and Kelly were still in the living room, sitting in the love seat across from him. He noticed Michael was just finishing rolling a joint. He then stared at Kelly and noticed her chin and forearms were covered in deep, purple bruises.

"My god Kelly, what happened?" Hank asked quickly, without thinking. Without even considering what kind of can of worms he had opened with Michael sitting right there. With his mind racing at a thousand miles an hour it occurred to him before she could answer that he had indeed possibly made a huge mistake.

"I got drunk as shit…I mean I was wasteder'n fuck. Blacked out, kept falling down and hit my chin on the counter.

Then I fell down the damn steps and hurt my arms. Don't tell anyone though…I don't want to be embarrassed. I just tell people Michael beat me." She said it all so matter of factly that she didn't even blink.

Hank realized then that he was in a place where people really did perceive the world in a very different way than he was used to. He kept hoping that she would come to some sort of epiphany after the acid kicked in. Then he realized that it had. He watched as her pupils dilated, she sat back and started staring at the trails she could see in the air as she waved her hands around in front of her.

"Wow," Michael kept repeating and breathing deeply as if he were thinking about the most profound thing a human had ever considered. Hank knew that Michael was high too, even if Michael was still unaware himself.

They sat in silence as they smoked the joint that Michael rolled, which was big enough to last a solid half hour with just the three of them smoking. Hank wondered how the party was going outside but figured it must be alright as the band was still playing. He closed his eyes and laid back in his seat, a large, leather sectional that was deep and sucked him into comfort instantly. He had always enjoyed tripping on acid and especially when he had the dank weed to smoke and keep himself chilled out. It wasn't long before he was conversing with Michael and Kelly with his eyes entirely closed, sipping off of the joint like it was a fine cognac. He got lost in the psychedelic display that played out on his eyelids. Everything was groovy and Hank was the most relaxed he had been in years.

As he started to giggle on the inside due to his extremely euphoric state he heard Kelly ask him, "do you realize you got real purdy eyes?"

Michael shot her a sideways glance that Hank could not see

but could definitely feel the sting of. He knew Michael to be the jealous type; the man often talked about it.

"Michael…I don't mean it like 'at," she explained. "I mean those baby blues sorta remind me of that guy that sings for Soundgarden."

Hank chuckled and opened his eyes up. Clearing his throat he said, "but his pupils ain't as big as these are they?"

They all had a good long laugh and it was all good vibes. There was joy and mirth in the air so thick it could almost be cut with a knife. It was definitely palpable to the three psychedelic rangers, tripping across the infinite scape of their own minds.

Eventually, the band stopped playing and Hank went out to the front porch to introduce the next band. The sun had set and it was dark, but with the stage lights set up on his porch, the full moon and the glow from the bonfire and pig roast, it was quite easy to see everyone and all that was going on. There were pretty girls hula hooping and people dancing, even after the music had ended. Everyone seemed as high to Hank as he was. The crowd was quite large for a field party and he couldn't be happier.

"How's everybody doin' tonight? Ya'll ready for some more jams? Ya'll ready to party?" He felt comfortable up there with the microphone even though he knew he had nothing to say. He could definitely see the appeal of being a musician. "Next up, from Lexington Kentucky, we have the one and only, the legendary, Funkzilla!"

Upon addressing the crowd and putting the mic back in its stand he finally spotted Amy, off to the side of the house. She was surrounded by a group of about twelve to fifteen people and he could see immediately that she had been busy all afternoon and evening being a good hostess to their numerous guests. He caught her attention after a few moments of staring at her. When he knew she was looking his way for sure he blew her a kiss. She caught it and blew him one back. Then in front of the whole group of people she was entertaining she lifted her shirt and exposed her tits to him. She had a half drunk bottle of Woodford Reserve bourbon in her hand and as she lifted her shirt she accidentally sloshed whiskey all over her breasts, making them glisten like an oiled up bikini model who had lost her top. He smiled ear to ear as he soaked in the sight of her large, dark areolas. He knew she wouldn't have spilled her "brown devil", as she called, it all over her exposed tits if she weren't drunk. Though tonight he was thankful that she was indeed plastered. As she lowered her shirt back down nobody in the group around her seemed to mind at all, but there were a few stares. Hank ignored those, after all, they were his wife's titties. Nobody else there could say that. He got an erection as his mind raced to ejaculating all over them as he had done so many times before, early in their romance, prior to his seizure medication taking away any sort of ability to maintain consistent erections. He never knew where or when they would come anymore, but he kept Amy as satisfied as any many could and he kept it as a point of pride that he did so with mostly just his tongue. And in his moment of clarity, so high he was visually and audibly hallucinating, he realized that it had been that way even before the car wreck. Before the seizures. It was his tongue that he used to pleasure her most. He knew his cock was inadequate to suit his bride. She was a full, strong woman, with a kinky streak a mile wide. Still, if he could smother her in orgasms it wouldn't matter to her where they came from, cock or tongue, and if he kept her satisfied he didn't feel any guilt about never bringing her to climax with his little dick. In fact, he had married her because she had been so nice to him about it.

He soon noticed that everyone in the group with Amy was staring at him and he was just standing on the porch with his jaw open and slack. He laughed at himself and realized that what to him had seemed like a long, deep process of thoughts and tangents had, in fact, occurred over the matter of only a few seconds.

"Goddamn, I am high as fuuuuck!" he thought to himself. "They don't know I'm trippin'." He then flashed Amy a few quick hand gestures to let her know he wanted to smoke some more weed and he wanted to smoke it with her. He went on into the house, leaving the porch just as Funkzilla was starting to set up their gear. As soon as he got back to the living room he found Michael and Kelly laughing hysterically at god only knew what. They were arm in arm, giggling like two school girls, in high pitched shrieks.

"Hank, your fish, it is hilarious. It knows the best jokes!" Michael said as he pointed at the larger of Hank's two aquariums. It was a fifty-five gallon tank but it had a fish in it that probably needed a hundred gallons at least all to itself, a big orange fish named Oscar.

"Oh, my, god…you are so damn high!" Hank joined in laughing at them, with them, around them, through them. He was just happy to be having so much fun. Then he heard it. SNAP! The sound of a tree branch shattering in half, but slightly muffled and with a sickening crunch. Then came the screams. He didn't know what or who he was hearing, couldn't make out the words they were using. All Hank knew was that whoever it was had gotten hurt bad and was in immeasurable agony. The band stopped playing. Other than the screams of pain there seemed to be no noise at all except for the sound of crickets chirping.

Hank tore through the house quickly, with a sense of purpose he hadn't often felt in his life. When he got out onto the porch he noticed that everyone and all the commotion seemed to be gathered around the bonfire. He ran over as fast as he could, across his yard that was as big as a field. Pushing his way to the front he saw one of his oldest pals from Lexington, Yuri Almeida, laying on his back next to the fire. He was gripping his knee and holding it up to his chest as his wife Ana Sophia plead with him to extend his leg out so they could get a look at his injury and assess the extent of the damage.

"Everyone back, give him some room to breathe! I'm a doctor!" a commanding voice addressed the crowd and everyone seemed to instantly obey without question, even Ana Sophia, who stepped back from her husband to see a tall, handsome stranger with olive skin, piercing blue eyes and thick and curly dark hair stride over to Yuri and crouch beside him.

After a few moments and some words exchanged that only Yuri and the doctor could hear Yuri got up and limped to his feet. He put one arm around the doctor and one arm around his wife and hopped between them one footed up to the house. Hank watched in awe, just dumbfounded, as the party began to get back underway. Everyone seemed satisfied that Yuri would be okay.

Hank stood for some time just staring into the fire. He didn't know how much time had passed. He just spaced out. His head felt uncomfortably clear and he wanted to return to the party. He spun hard on his right heel and started toward the house. Before he even took a full step he knew something was very, very wrong. The party seemed to have disappeared entirely. The house was oriented to the East instead of the

South and although it looked quite a bit different he somehow knew it was the same house. He stumbled backwards a step, thought he might stumble into the fire and spun around again, the opposite direction. He fell right down where the fire should have been but found instead he fell on cold, damp ground. As he looked up he noticed the barn was in the same place. At least something seemed familiar. He laughed at himself sitting there in the dark, in the yard, so high he was probably just sitting right in the fire and didn't even know it. As he stood up a chill went down his spine. He felt cold and looked up and saw the moon become obscured by clouds. A thick hazy fog crept over the fields and across the yard. As it enveloped him Hank got the suspicion that he was in danger. He immediately felt like he should be running and he did not ignore his instinct. He felt almost silly, running from nothing. Still, he ran towards the house as fast as his legs and mind could carry him. He heard a growling over the sounds of his footfalls. An animalistic, voracious growl that betrayed a murderous intent. Whatever it was it was close, it was chasing him and it intended that he be its dinner. That was all Hank knew. As his palms sweated profusely and his heart pounded nearly out of his chest he tried to stay focused on survival. He felt as if he were being outpaced rapidly, but still, he chanced a glance over his shoulder. Not much more than the blur of two crimson eyes. The eyes he had seen on the first night he spent here in Gravel Switch, he was sure of it. There was a long howling as if from a mutated, dying wolf choking on a thousand locusts. Hank prepared to meet his maker and let a dribble of piss out of his tiny penis, soaking through his pants.

Then as if by miracle the beast bounded right past him as if he weren't even there and headed straight for the house. To Hank's surprise, a volley of musket balls came from the windows of his house, maybe a dozen. He knew the sound of the civil war era weapons being fired. He had attended a few civil war reenactments as a kid, had even gotten to fire a musket once at camp. He flinched, too late, at the thought of being struck. He tucked, almost fetal, as he heard the projectiles tearing through the flesh of whatever it was ahead of him. It seemed unfazed other than being slightly annoyed.

Hank chanced his first good look at the thing to see a wretched creature straight out of his nightmares. It seemed to be about the same mass as a grizzly bear but it looked much like a jackal, or a hyena…definitely not a wolf. Hank immediately noticed that it had much longer, lankier legs than either of those creatures though. This was unlike anything he had ever seen before. It had a tail of thick, shaggy fur that seemed to split into two halfway down and Hank could not tell if that was natural to the abominable beast or if it had been split as if by some injury. Its claws were as straight razors folded back into their handles, each one an implement of death, together a nightmare. Something about its head and the way it moved it seemed to reveal that the thing had an intelligence at least equal to that of a person and far beyond that of any of the animals it resembled. It appeared to take in everything it saw, smelled and heard all at once and process it rapidly. The face was elongated like a shaggy horse's face, but the ears were long like a jackrabbit and the thing had ram like horns curling out from behind them. Its eyes flashed with red fury as it stood aloft on its hindquarters and roared another hideous howl into the thick fog and the cold night.

Hank decided to do something daring. He ran around the thing, which still did not seem to notice him in the slightest. He smelled its rank breathe he got so close, a foul mix of death and rot. He ran for the house, as fast and as deliberately as he could. Every stride a specific effort to get to Amy. Whatever this thing was a few boards and some bricks were not going to protect her or anyone else in the house from it.

When he got to the front door he went to open it and his hand went right through it as if it weren't even there at all. It seemed as if he were incorporeal, a ghost or spirit, incapable of interacting with the physical world, yet bound to observe it. He stole his fear away and walked right through the front door. As he did so he felt a terrible cold but that passed instantly. He was in the foyer of his house, yet not his house. It appeared as he thought it might have appeared in the eighteen hundreds. As he walked from the foyer into the living room he heard voices in a whisper.

"Captain...I do not think we are going to survive this night. That thing has hunted us all day and night. Bullets do not concern it. Nor do bayonets. I have no doubt that this thing is a spawn of hell sent to punish us all for our trepidations on this earth," Hank overheard a man with a thick southern accent. As he fully entered the living room he saw a dozen Rebel civil war soldiers gathered there. All in various states of duress and all obviously at least a little wounded. Some were obviously severely wounded. Every man in the room other than Hank was scathed in some way. He knew immediately that none of them could see him, they probably couldn't hear him either. He tried walking through one just for fun and found it much more uncomfortable than walking through the door. Still, it only lasted a moment.

He walked into the kitchen as the soldiers considered how they might prevail over the beast in the yard. It was there that he saw something that truly shocked him. Lying face down on the floor was a young black woman in a white dress and apron, with a blue bonnet. She seemed to be dead and it appeared to have happened recently. There were pots and pans and plates laying all about her. She was covered in flour and sugar and there seemed to be several broken jars around on the floor. There had obviously been a struggle. He noticed her dress was ripped in several places and pushed up to her waist, past her hips. Her legs were spread apart and as Hank examined her body he got embarrassed at himself for letting his gaze linger a little too long on her. He couldn't help but think how beautiful her skin was, how smooth it seemed and how warm and inviting her womanly pleasures must have been before she died. As he regained his composure from the shock of it all he realized first that he too might be dead and also that she appeared to have been brutally raped and murdered. He gasped at the thoughts, almost retching at the realization that he had just sexualized both a rape victim and a corpse in his mind.

He crouched beside her and in desperation, he began to cry. Grabbing his knees he rocked back and forth, weeping like a baby. "That poor thing…those fucked up soldiers…oh my fucking god…" he kept repeating to himself, as Michael had repeated "Wow" over and over earlier that night when he had first felt the effects of LSD. "Was it even the same day?" Hank wondered if he might have been…in what, Civil War times? … for much longer than it seemed.

Then Hank heard a voice that he was sure was directed at him, "Psst. Psst. Hey, mistuh…look at me mistuh…We gotta get outta here, right now." Hank looked up and saw a middle-aged black man, maybe forty years old, dressed in shabby cotton clothes that were filthy and worn full of holes. He had no shoes and a rope belt. He had a jacket that looked scratchier than a burlap bag. In his right hand, he had a pistol and in his left hand an unlit torch. He had the back door wide open and was leaning into the kitchen, staring directly at Hank.

"We gots to go, Hank," he said matter of factly. "This house is about to burn to the damn ground. Now help me get Matilda outta here."

To his surprise, the man entered the kitchen stealthily, put the pistol in his waistband and set the torch down outside the back door. Hank found that Matilda was one thing he could actually grasp onto physically. He grabbed her arms and the other man got her legs and they rushed her out the back door. They carried her across the yard, out to the buildings Hank thought of as the slave quarters. It occurred to him right then and there that these were once the occupants of those mysterious buildings in his yard. They laid her body down inside the closer of the two shacks on a cot inside, the only piece of furniture in it. Then Hank followed the man back to the house.

The man closed the back door, locking it from the outside by securing it shut with a heavy chain Hank which had failed to notice was lying right next to the door. Then the man lit the torch and started setting fire to the building. He started several small fires along the base of the outside walls, just above the foundation.

"What is your name?" Hank asked a little sheepishly.

"I'm Sheridan...Sheridan Davis. Matilda was my wife. Those damn confederate bastards raped her and killed her. I arrived just in time to see through the window. You, Hank Ramsey, have helped me with my revenge. I will not forget that," the man said in a detached way as if nothing that had happened had really gotten to him emotionally.

"How do you know my name? How am I here?" Hank asked.

"We are between life and death, caught up in a place where those worlds collide. Time here is meaningless Hank. Space is meaningless. We are always and forever trapped in this here place, in this torment, over and over 'til time itself stops. Some of us recognize it, like me. Others are clueless to their fate every damn time…" Sheridan trailed off. Hank knew that Sheridan understood he was dead; and long so.

Still, as they talked the small fires had turned into a conflagration. The house was going up quick. Two rebels came to the back door, found it locked and as they tried to kick it open met a bloody end as Sheridan shot the first one through the window, striking him square in the eye. As he fell to the ground Sheridan reached through the shattered glass pane of the back door and stuck a knife into the second man's neck. He left the blade in as the soldier fell back gurgling and spurting out blood. Just like that, in the blink of an eye, the man had easily dispatched two Confederate soldiers. Then Sheridan took Hank's hand and led him around the front of the house.

He said, "This is my favorite part," just as the front door flew open and three soldiers poured out of the house, staggering and coughing from smoke inhalation. The first one came running across the yard, right toward where Hank had fallen into what should have been a fire pit but turned out instead to be a walking nightmare in the nineteenth century. As the first soldier ran Hank saw those red eyes come charging out from the barn, making a direct line of interception for the soldier. The thing was upon him in just a few bounds; howling its terrible, spine piercing howl. The soldier trembled, barely able to raise his weapon, which immediately backfired. He stumbled back as the beast sniffed him deeply, seeming to feed on his fear of it. Then with a lightning quick flash, it swiped its clawed front paw across the belly of the soldier, opening the boy up five times. Each claw a scimitar cutting in from the side, then a gaff hook drawing intestines out and flinging them casually on the ground. The boy lay there suffering and whimpering, dying quickly as the last thing he heard was that hellish howl and the screams of his friends burning to death.

The other two soldiers that made it out of the house had only two choices. Charge the damned thing and try to win a futile fight, or burn to death like their other comrades. Choosing to fight was agreed upon by the two men with a nonverbal nod. After all, they were soldiers. Win or lose. Live or die. Their lot in life was to fight.

With a pathetic Rebel Yell that was as good as the two boys could muster they charged the field with all the strength and adrenalin that comes with facing certain death. The beast just stood there. It almost seemed to not even notice them. Then as they got within melee range with their bayonets they both fired, right into its face. One musket ball seemed to simply disappear but the other struck home in the best possible way and put out the right eye, of the accursed thing. It reared back on its haunches and came down hard, crashing its whole weight into the first of the two young southern boys, who splattered like a tomato under its strength. The other boy stabbed the thing in the chest with his bayonet. It laughed at him in a guttural, sinister voice. Then its head reared back, its jaws distended and it snapped the head clean off the boy. In a flash it struck, like a viper, its large square teeth tearing the head off as easily as a knife through butter. Hank was shocked at the brutality. The body remained standing as a crimson gout sprayed out of the neck, shooting the man's life force several feet into the air as the beast bathed in blood, still standing in the puddle that was all that remained of the soldier who was splattered.

Hank had never seen such gore in his life. He had never smelled death up close and personal before. Had never smelled the bile, the blood, the excrement. He was sickened beyond belief, but more than a physical sickness he was sick with himself for enjoying what he saw. After what those men did to poor Matilda…he had no sympathy for anything that happened to them.

He then noticed that Sheridan was staring at the beast and it was staring at him.

They seemed to be communicating in some way that Hank could not understand. Then it bounded off back toward the barn. When it got there it turned and stared back at Hank and Sheridan, this time with one glowing red eye and not two.

Everything went black. Hank lost his balance and collapsed. He lost consciousness. He awoke in a hospital bed, a heart monitor the only thing to keep him company. As he tried to get his bearings a nurse entered the room.

"Oh, good, you're awake now. We had to sedate you heavily. You had one of the worst seizures I've ever seen. Your wife's been worried sick about you. She just went to the cafeteria for coffee…hasn't left your side 'til a few minutes ago. I'll let her know you are awake now," the nurse seemed to talk faster than Hank could comprehend.

"Seizure…seizure…I had a seizure," he said to himself repeatedly, trying to come to terms with all he had experienced. Trying to form words despite the medication that was numbing his brain.

6

OLD FRIENDS

*A*fter Yuri hurt himself jumping over the fire a doctor that Amy had invited to the party had attended to his injury. He had suggested that Yuri go get his knee checked out, that it could be sprained pretty bad but was probably just hyperextended. He gave Yuri a shot of Demerol for the pain, as well as just plain giving him a bottle of hydrocodone with at least two hundred and fifty pills in it. They were the thirty-milligram ones too, not the cheap ones. Ana Sophia knew he had just handed her thousands of dollars worth of pills when he gave her the bottle for Yuri. He suggested she eat as many as she needed too, in case her nerves were shot.

As they had gotten Yuri settled in the living room, laid out on the sectional couch with his leg propped up with an ice pack on it, Hank had been going through a seizure the likes of which they had never seen. He had even fallen right into the fire and doctor Jared came to the rescue. He had to be rushed to the hospital due to a severe reaction to some drug he had taken before his epileptic fit and also to be treated for burns. Where he fell into the fire he managed to burn much of his hair off.

Ana Sophia was thankful that word came from the hospital and Hank was doing okay. With both Hank and Yuri out of the woods, so to speak, Ana Sophia finally began to relax. Amy suggested she take a shower, slip into something comfortable and zonk out in their master bedroom. Amy was planning on staying the night at the hospital as she knew Hank was going to be there a while, undergoing various tests and brain scans. CAT and MRI among them, but they usually did other tests as well. All in all, he was never just in and out of the hospital and this was by far the worst seizure Hank ever had. She didn't tell the staff at the hospital that Hank was high on acid when he had his seizure but had let Ana Sophia know so that she and Yuri could know what was really happening with Hank.

Ana Sophia took a shower in the only working bathroom in the massive house. The pipes squeaked loudly and groaned as if they didn't want to produce any water but eventually they poured forth a grimy smelling, sticky fluid that vaguely resembled the tap water she was used to in Lexington. Having grown up in Brazil she had wondered how America had such shitty water. Still, the shower was calming and relaxed her a great deal. She hoped Yuri was okay and felt reassured that Jared seemed to think he was fine. But there was such a loud noise when he landed. It sounded like a tree branch snapping. She remembered him flying through the air, right over the fire, as he'd done several times that night. He was always doing silly physical things and joking around, he was very athletic, but something seemed to happen. She knew when she saw the hand of evil work upon the earth. Especially when it targeted someone she loved. And this situation reeked of exactly that. She felt a cold rush up her spine right as he jumped and then she saw him hit an invisible wall while mid-air. He hit an immovable nothingness and all of his forward motion simply stopped and he was slammed directly to the ground as if grabbed by some invisible hand and thrown forcefully at the earth. Nobody else that she knew of seemed to notice the details of what happened. Everyone else was high on at least one drug or another, but Ana Sophia was paying close attention to her husband and she had never been high in her entire life. What she saw made her question whether or not someone had slipped something into her drink.

She climbed out of the shower only after all the hot water had run out, which was only about ten minutes, which was disappointing to her as she had really wanted to relax. She put on a pair of Amy's pajamas and proceeded to the bedroom where Amy had set Yuri up on the bed with his ice pack and pillows under his leg. Yuri was so doped up he could barely keep his eyes open, yet he was still awake and greeted his wife with an indecipherable slur as she entered the room.

Ana Sophia smiled at him and crawled into bed next to him after toweling her hair dry and turning the light off. She kissed her husband and they both found sleep quickly and easily. She hadn't slept that deeply in months. This was the first night that she and Yuri had been away from their kids in as long.

Still, she awoke in the middle of the night when a loud bang upstairs startled her. It sounded like something as large as a person fell from ceiling to floor upstairs and it shook the whole house. When she woke it was with such a start that she sat bolt upright immediately and reflexively. She was sweating profusely and yet she was ice cold. She gained her bearings a bit before she noticed that Yuri was not in bed with her anymore. She figured he must be in the kitchen as it looked like the light was on down the hall. After a moment he appeared in the doorway, breathing heavily. He didn't seem to be bothered by the injury at all. Ana Sophia figured that he must have taken his ice pack into the kitchen and found the swelling had gone down. Now he was walking good, but tomorrow it would likely be bothersome. Still, she patted the bed next to her and invited him to come back to sleep. She had forgotten all about the banging sound that woke her up and just wanted Yuri to rejoin her, but he stood in the doorway, just breathing heavily. She found after a minute or two that she was both slightly disturbed and extremely turned on. He finally approached and she was excited with the anticipation of just grabbing him and forcing him inside her. She and her husband had a deep sexual connection and she knew it would be no problem to get him to fuck her. Even injured he was usually horny all the time and ready and willing to make love to her at the drop of a hat. He may have grown up in Kentucky, but Yuri was Brazilian ethnically and who better to pleasure a Brazilian man than a Brazilian woman? She could think of no one.

As he approached the bed she felt his energy was primal and overwhelming. She could feel his presence like a hand on her back, or as he got closer, a slap in the face. Something wasn't right with him. He just stood there, breathing deeply, like an animal. Then out of nowhere, he climbed into the bed and right on top of her. He pulled her hair hard and she purred like a cat. He climbed on top of her tearing away the buttons on the borrowed pajamas forcefully and easily with his mouth as he ravenously searched for her breasts. Spitting the buttons out he took her nipple into his mouth and sucked so hard she thought it would come off. Then he bit. She screamed in horror and ecstasy.

He tore off his pants and hers in just a couple of seconds. Her musk was potent smelling, she was so wet and turned on that she felt like a high school girl. He flipped her over and spit into his hand, forcefully. He was much more rough with her than usual and because of that, she found herself coming to orgasm quickly. Then in the midst of ecstasy, his demeanor changed and was diametrically different. She hated it immediately. It was violent, brutal and violating. She was scared.

Yuri began to laugh in a voice that Ana Sophia did not recognize as he thrust into her ass, immediately putting in the entirety of his penis and brutally pounding away. She gasped in pain but could not scream out as he had her face buried in a pillow. He punched her hard with his other hand in the back and sides. She tried to roll over, to get a breath. She couldn't. She was trying to struggle, but her strength was fading.

In desperation, she reached out for the nightstand next to the bed. She knew there was a lamp, an old rotary phone and several other odds and ends on it. She clawed at the table with her left hand, all the while gasping for a breath. Adrenalin coursed through her as she fought to stay alive, helped her to ignore the anal rape and furious, hellbent punches she was enduring. That was secondary, she would deal with that if she could just get a breath. Even as she struggled in her desperate last attempt, even as the adrenalin made her nauseous, she found herself losing consciousness. Then her tiny fingers found what she immediately recognized as scissors. When she knew what she held it gave her the second wind to attack, to save her life and her dignity.

Turning and thrusting in one motion she heard a loud yelp as the scissors in her hand tore through flesh. He let go of her and fell backward, his swollen cock dislodging from her wounded anus. She turned over fully, sitting upright and clutching the covers over her nakedness with one hand while gesturing aggressively with the scissors.

"What the fuck Yuri?!" she screamed as loud as she could at him, tears streaming down her face.

"Ain't no Yuri here girl," a vicious growl came from his mouth in an accent that sounded both Asian and country bumpkin hillbilly at once. "Just yo' daddy girl. Just Quan. An you done stabbed me in the knee. Gonna have'ta go see the doctor in the mo'nin'. We done been through this girl, we done been through this." He grabbed his belt and began beating her, whooping and hollering at her the whole time. She dropped the scissors quickly, unable to defend against the ferocity of the blows. He beat her for ten minutes straight and she had only the blankets to protect her naked body from his immense strength. She knew this man was not her husband, yet he used Yuri's body. He tore the blankets off of her and backhanded her hard. Ana Sophia's tiny skull hit the headboard and knocked her out.

What she immediately recognized as several minutes later she came to. Stunned still by his actions and the daze she was in, she found herself alone in that bedroom. She got her clothes on, those buttonless pajamas Amy had given her what seemed like a century ago. It caused her immeasurable pain just to move as she was bruised from head to toe. Ana Sophia knew that if she survived the ordeal she would be black and blue for months.

After taking a moment to breathe deeply she ran through the house in a panic, just wanting away. She knew if she could make it to her car that there was a spare key in a magnetic box stuck to the frame under the back left tire. She focused on that as if keeping straight the minute details of her escape would make or break her chances of living through the situation. To some extent, she was not wrong. She heard a scratching noise coming from the back of the house when she first exited the bedroom and entered the massive hallway that led to freedom or death. It sounded to her much like cat's claws on wood. Giant cat's claws as the noise was so loud. Feeling like a mouse she ran as fast as she could for the front door, in the dark tripping on a rug in the foyer and falling loudly only feet from the portal to freedom. She got up as fast as she could, grabbed the doorknob and threw the front door open. The coast looked clear and she was glad she had chosen to run away from the terrible noises although her car was closer to the back door. She threw herself through the doorway onto the front porch with the full intent of sprinting as fast as she could to her car. Her legs went into high gear and propelled her faster than she had ever run before.

Ana Sophia felt a searing, immeasurable pain cut through her torso. Her legs still kicking as she was lifted into the air. Yuri, or rather Quan using his body, had been standing to the right of the front door against the building in the shadows. As she threw the front door open and dashed through it to what she thought was her escape he had spun and shoved a rusty, antique pitchfork through her side, piercing her with three of the four miniature spears that had grown jagged and brown with a century's worth of age and neglect.

Ana Sophia yelped as her husband, possessed by the madman, flung her body off of the pitchfork and down the front steps, onto the front yard. He bounded down the steps after her. She could only roll over onto her back and spit up blood which was coming ever more rapidly up her throat and out of her mouth. She could only guess where he had punctured her, but as he was upon her again it did not matter. He stabbed her dozens of times, all in the chest and stomach. She died in horrible agony, her last words, "Yuri...please...stop," before she was only coughing up blood.

The last thing that Ana Sophia saw was the reflection of two glowing red eyes next to her car. As darkness overtook her they came closer. She could smell the stench of rot on the hotness of its breath.

"Stay away from my wife!" she heard in her husband's voice. His true voice. Ana Sophia was comforted to know that the last thing she heard was her husband's voice. But she didn't die so quickly. It took her half a minute before her consciousness was gone from the world entirely. What had been words became screams of absolute agony. She felt a weight bearing down on top of her mutilated body, knowing that her husband had suffered terribly as she did. When the darkness overcame her she was quick to embrace it.

7

THE AFTERPARTY AND THE DREAM

The next morning Amy returned home, Hank still in the hospital. He had a series of MRI's and other time-consuming appointments that day and Amy wanted to go home and take a nap. She was looking forward to smoking a bowl and chilling with her friends Yuri and Ana Sophia. It had been a long while since she had really spent any quality time with her friends. She had been Ana Sophia's roommate in college at the University of Kentucky and had been maid of honor at their wedding. Ana Sophia had always been there for her, like nobody else, and Yuri had known Hank since they were boys at Tate's Creek Junior High School. As much as she felt bad leaving Hank alone at the hospital she knew his mother would be there later that afternoon and his sister would probably stop by. Jared would be on duty at the hospital later that night and had promised to check up on Hank. She realized that "if it weren't for Jared...well", she shuddered to think, "Hank might not have made it."

After she had driven for nearly two hours she began to feel

exhausted. Staying up all night, talking with doctors and nurses, holding Hank's hand through the worst of his seizure, had all taken their toll on her mind and body. Her muscles had become saturated with stress and she seemed to lose her focus driving, which she knew was not safe out on those central Kentucky curvy roads.

Still, she managed to make it home in one piece but became overwhelmingly panicked as she made it to the end of the driveway to see the Almeida's laid out on her front yard. As she parked the car her mind raced with all of the possibilities of what could have happened. She practically jumped from the driver's seat, forgetting to close her door. Amy ran as fast as she could across the front yard and right up to the Almeidas. Yuri was hunched over Ana Sophia, collapsed on top of her. Their bodies intertwined in an island floating alone in a sea of blood that soaked the ground and as Amy stepped closer her shoe was covered nearly to the ankle in the thick, sticky, red coagulation of their spilled live's essence. Yuri's back was shredded to pieces, his shirt disintegrated by some unknown slashing imple- ment. His form huddled over his wife's immediately revealed that he had died, in vain, trying to protect her. Amy could see pieces of his ribcage as most of the flesh had been stripped from his back. She noticed bite marks all over his body. Then her gaze turned to Ana Sophia, her good friend, her roommate in college. A woman who was like a sister to her.

As she looked down in shock and horror at Ana Sophia's body it finally dawned on Amy. That her friend laid beneath her husband and was wearing the pajamas Amy had loaned her the night before. Amy began to feel dizzy. A sudden nausea came over her and she vomited up everything in her stomach. This was way more than she could handle. She began to look around frantically for some sort of clue as to what had happened. Laying in the grass, some twenty feet from the bodies of her dear friends, Amy saw a pitchfork. It was covered in blood and she knew that Yuri must have used it to try to protect them from whatever wild animal or animals it was who did such a wretched thing.

"My god...how did this happen?" she asked the sky as she shook her fist at the clouds. At the god she did not believe in. Tears streaking down her cheeks as fresh ones flooded into her dark blue eyes. Amy collapsed right there on the ground, into the blood, right next to the bodies, and sobbed.

It was over an hour before she was able to collect herself enough to stand up again. She was snapped back to reality by the sound of flies buzzing about the bodies. Immediately upon her return to reality and rational thought, Amy pulled her car into the yard and positioned it so that nothing could be seen from the road, even by someone using binoculars. She wasn't going to take any chances. Next, she called Jared, who told her to wait for him on the front porch after getting cleaned up, that he would take care of everything.

Jared didn't take more than ten minutes to arrive and Amy was still in the shower when he pulled down the driveway in a black Ford SUV that she had never seen before. Although the windows were tinted she could tell that there were at least three people in the vehicle. She became very uncomfortable at the thought of anyone, even Jared, knowing what had happened. That she had two dead bodies in her yard.

Most people would have just called the police and had an ambulance come and proceed as normal. But then again most people didn't have several hundred marijuana plants growing in their house upstairs. Amy couldn't take the chance that Hank would go to jail. He wouldn't make it in there with his epilepsy. She would do whatever it took to keep this extreme situation from becoming any more of a mess than it already was. She would make a deal with the goddamn devil if she had to. Nothing else mattered. Just getting those bodies out of there. Just going back to life as normal.

Jared hardly said anything to her at all. He just got out of the car and was already working on cleaning things up when Amy came out on the front porch, still toweling her hair dry. He said nothing more than, "Don't worry about this. We will make it look like a car accident. The car will be burned. The county sheriff and the coroner already know the situation and they are with us...thangs out here are....well it just works different."

He turned to get back to the mess and with his back to Amy said, "Go on back in the house. Smoke a bowl. Take a valium. I won't be more than an hour. When I get back then we have a lot to talk about."

"Ok. And thanks...I really don't know what to say," she turned and walked back inside. She got out Hank's biggest bong and packed a solid eighth ounce of their best cannabis into the bowl, lit it and took a hit so big she choked for a minute straight. Coughing like a high school kid taking her first toke Amy laughed at herself after she regained her composure. After all the months they had lived in that house and after all the freaky shit she had experienced Amy just couldn't believe that something that violent could happen to her friends. It all seemed so surreal. She just couldn't believe they were dead. The thing that got to Amy the most about it was the thought of their children growing up without parents. She shuddered again, took another bong hit and laid down on the couch, drifting into a deep sleep easily and quickly.

Amy awoke sometime later to Jared gently shaking her by the arm. She awoke slowly and groggily, wiping drool from her mouth. She still felt a bit in a daze but was glad to see Jared. His face was a welcome sight after a day of such horrors. She gazed deep into his dark eyes before speaking.

"How did it go?" she asked timidly. Afraid of the answer no matter what it was.

"Alright. The sheriff should be finding the crash any time now. The official story is that they got lost out here deep in the country, hit a tree, car caught fire and they burned. Coyotes will explain the bites all over them. Local coroner will corroborate the story," he sounded deadpan as if recalling something extremely mundane. He quickly realized that he was being detached and attempted to comfort her. "Amy, I'm really sorry for your loss. I know you were very close with them."

"Thanks, Jared. God…I appreciate everything you've done. If it weren't for you and how connected you are out here… well…we'd be going to prison. Let me give you some weed for now. It is the least I can do." She pulled a tray out from beneath the couch she had been sleeping on. It had a wooden box on it in which Hank kept his most choice buds. It was the best of the best, marijuana flowers that should have been in High Times magazine. She opened the lid and pulled out half of what was in there and gave it to Jared. It probably amounted to two ounces.

"Thanks a lot, Amy. I sure do appreciate it. But…well there is going to be a steep price to pay for what went down today. A lot of people had to look the other way, fabricate an untrue narrative and paint certain pictures. Others had to handle things and get their hands dirty, cleaning the mess up, like myself. I didn't want you involved with these people Amy. They're Cornbread Mafia…"

He went to continue but she interrupted him with a loud guffaw. She laughed and laughed almost hysterically. She thought he was joking. After almost a minute she realized that he was not.

"That's just what they call themselves Amy…but the point is they don't fuck around. These are not people to cross and certainly not people to mess with or owe any favors to. Unfortunately, they were the only people to turn to for such an extreme situation," he said to her while gazing deeply into her eyes, trying to convey a sense of urgency to her that she seemed not to be getting.

"I see. Well, whatever it takes. I'd pretty much make a deal with the devil to make this mess go away. God…Hank doesn't even know. Maybe I shouldn't even tell him?" she pondered, half to Jared, half to herself.

"We have to tell Hank. He's going to grow us a shitload of clones for next season. He's as good as it gets at cutting clones and he has the best strain around. Next year your all's strain will be the commercial outdoor that Marion county runs on. That's the plan at least. Hope y'all can handle that. They want ten thousand cuttings rooted, ready to go by April. I told them that was a steep order for anyone to fill, but they really didn't care."

"Jared, what happens if we can't come through on that order?" she asked, again afraid of the answer no matter what it was. Amy knew that cloning marijuana plants by taking a cutting from a mother plant and rooting it, much as tomato growers do, was Hank's specialty. She knew that he had a near one hundred percent success rate with rooting cuttings, but she also knew that ten thousand clones were much more than he had ever done by an order of magnitude. She also immediately began to worry what kind of space ten thousand marijuana plants were going to take up in her house, no matter how small they were.

"I really don't know, but it won't be pretty. Basically, it ain't an option. It just ain't, so go on and get that notion right out of yer head right now. This is probably do or die," as he laid it all out for her Amy found herself slightly amused. She had always been attracted to danger and this was as dangerous as it could get.

They sat mostly in silence for a few hours, listening to music. Jared called into work to stay with Amy and she was super thankful, not just to have someone there in such a stressful time, but that it was Jared. She tried to give him every indication that she was attracted to him. It had been so long since Hank had satisfied her that sometimes she would tell herself that she no longer cared if she hurt him. Amy looked at herself more as his caretaker than his lover and it wasn't in her nature to hold on to feelings of guilt. Jared was right here in front of her and she knew he wanted her as much as she wanted him.

After long awkward silences and several rounds of bong hits of Hank's weed, Amy leaned over and began kissing Jared. He did not resist, but he did not respond as she thought he would. He sat there, neither accepting nor rejecting her. This made Amy furious. She lost her cool fast and shoved her tongue past his lips, taking his head in her hands. He could not play coy any longer, kissing her back passionately.

After making out for half an hour they just sat and held each other. After holding each other they did more bong hits. "Hank is impotent. I haven't been fucked properly in years. It is his seizure medication. It basically numbs his brain and well… the brain don't work, the dick don't work. He goes down on me a lot, but even when he was at his best…I was never satisfied," she found herself confessing to him.

He seemed to take it all in even though he said nothing. He

just held her tighter. Amy hadn't felt that comfortable in years. Not since she had first met Hank. She felt like she could tell him anything and he wouldn't judge her. She moved his arms off of her, stood up, took his hand and led him into the bedroom.

He followed, silently, but intensely. She could feel his pulse quicken as she opened the bedroom door. She threw Jared onto the bed and climbed on top of him.

Hours later, late into the night, they both awoke in each other's arms naked. The sound of a car coming down the driveway bringing them both out of the deep post-coital slumber that they had fallen into. They both jumped up quickly and scrambled to get dressed and to the living room where they could casually play off that they had been doing bong hits for hours.

Just as they were getting believably situated Hank entered the front door. He came through the foyer looking happy and chipper as if nothing had happened the night before. He entered the living room and blew Amy a kiss and walked over to Jared and leaning over the back of the couch Jared was on gave him a deep hug.

"Thank you, brother. You saved me. You saved my fuckin' life," Hank gushed.

"I just gave you a shot of valium Hank. Anyone could have done that," Jared downplayed the situation, trying to be humble but slightly annoying Hank.

"Hank...honey...I have some really bad news. We have a lot to talk about," Amy rained on the parade. Hank immediately knew by the tone she used that something was extremely wrong. Something world shattering had occurred in his absence. He didn't want to know but knew that it was inevitable and braced himself for impact.

Amy patted the couch next to her, motioning for Hank to sit with them. She packed him a bong of their best weed and recounted everything that had happened from the moment she had gotten home up to her and Jared doing bong hits on the couch, which is where she left the story and left Hank with the impression that he had come home during that moment. She and Jared both played off their lovemaking with icy stone hearts. Amy knew Hank would be oblivious; and if he found out? Well, it was an extremely stressful situation, he'd have to understand. Part of her didn't care if he did or not as she remembered the passion she had recently shared with Jared.

As Amy wrestled with all the emotions that were flooding her heart and clouding her mind as Hank sat on the couch, stunned, unable to process the deaths of Yuri and Ana Sophia. He put his head in his hands and wept. Amy rubbed his back as he cried until he had no more tears. His best friend on earth had died in his yard, along with his wife. Hank was shocked that he didn't have a seizure with such stressful news. He felt like nothing in the world mattered anymore and in that moment, having shed his tears, hid his heart behind a stone wall of nihilism. He gave Jared a stern look, asking without words what it was that was expected of him. He knew Amy didn't clean up the mess alone and that there would be a toll required of him.

"Hank, there is a steep price to pay for what we had to do for you all today," Jared deadpanned. "They're gonna need ten thousand clones."

"Not gonna be a problem at all," Hank was overconfident. "No problem whatsoever," he reiterated, half to himself, with a fake bravado in his voice. The type he only used when he was in denial and trying to convince himself of something.

He packed another bong hit and before long it was so late

they were all feeling the effects of the marijuana and could barely keep their eyes open. Hank and Amy retired to the master bedroom and set Jared up on the couch with some blankets and a thick goose down pillow.

Hank slept easily enough. Amy, on the other hand, kept tossing and turning all night, thinking of Jared in the living room, on the couch. Thinking of the passionate lovemaking they had done only hours before, right where she lay with Hank. It was a type of torture that she was not used to feeling. Eventually, Hank was snoring deeply and she risked a trip out to see Jared. She walked out of her bedroom and down the back hallway into the kitchen. She turned on the light switch and got a glass of water, making just enough noise to let Jared know someone was awake in case he was not sleeping too deeply.

Amy walked back to her bedroom, this time going through the front of the house, deliberately crossing through the living room. She just wanted to be close with Jared again. To feel his strong arms around her. She felt so safe there, unlike with Hank. When she got close to the couch she could see that he wasn't there. She turned on a lamp that was on the end table next to the couch and saw he had left them a note, explaining that he had been called into work. She felt her heart sag in her chest a bit, before she picked herself back up with the thought, "'I'm sleeping with a doctor!"

She curled up on the couch and went back to sleep. Smelling the blanket deeply, inhaling Jared's musk. Her mind raced through the dream world. She was not one to remember her dreams often, but this one she would never forget. It was one of those nightmares where she was no longer sure if she were awake or asleep, but knew that either way she was dreaming.

She woke up shaking, but her house was not quite the same. It seemed like it was no longer a relic of the nineteenth century but it was fresh and new, yet still of that time. She wandered around in a daze, not recognizing any of the items or furniture occupying the living room. It was as if she had stepped through a time machine.

Eventually, she became panicked. Frantically she ran through the house trying to find something that looked even remotely familiar. Everything was a relic of a bygone age. She stopped in the hallway, outside of her room and began to sob. After what she assumed must have been several minutes, although she could not tell if it had been days or hours, Amy heard a loud thud from upstairs and the whole house shook as if hit by a heavyweight.

As out of place as she felt curiosity got the best of Amy. She was across the hall from the stairwell and all she had to do was open the door and ascend the stairs to find the answer to her curiosity. Still, she walked slowly and deliberately. Taking each step with both feet before climbing to the next.

She got to the top of her ascent and found a room unlike any that she knew to be in her house. It looked much like a ballroom and was dominated by a large crystal chandelier. The wallpaper seemed like it was from an old apothecary; the ones in western movies like her grandparents used to watch. The floor was painted white and was dominated by a colorful Persian rug inlaid with intricate patterns of sparrows and branches. A long serving table of shiny oak ran the distance of the entire back wall. Tied off to the wall was a rope that ran alongside the chain which held the chandelier aloft. There was a body on the floor, beneath the chandelier with a broken noose around its neck. It was a man by the look of it, wearing tattered rags evocative of the nineteenth century and a much simpler time.

Amy's pulse quickened as she realized that the loud noises she heard coming from the upstairs were the sounds of this man's body falling from the chandelier and hitting the floor. "How long have you been up here?" she thought to herself, although she could feel her lips move.

"He hung himself. He deserved it for what he did to me," a voice as cold as the grave came from behind Amy and although she was startled it seemed to paralyze her with fear. She felt ice run up her spine.

She spun around to find a ghostly apparition; see-through and seething at the edges with an ectoplasm who's astral essence was not fit for the confines of the physical world. A young woman in a Victorian dress, tattered but obviously well made and expensive, her face a menagerie of features, stood before Amy. Amy could not tell if this young woman was African American, Caucasian, Asian, Native American or a mix of several things. She only knew that the person was no longer alive and was not exactly physically present.

Amy had always wanted to see a ghost. She had often wondered at the fanciful tales other kids would tell at school recess and lunch. Tales about their own experiences with the supernatural. She never believed any of them because she had never known anything of the sort herself. She had always figured that the sight of such a horror would be quite a life-changing experience and in that moment Amy knew she was not wrong.

With her mind racing a thousand miles per hour Amy instinctively stepped backward, then took another step and another. Trying desperately to put distance between herself and that weird spirit before her she did not notice the body on the floor any longer until it was too late. Amy tripped over the corpse and fell backward onto her back. She hit the floor with a loud thump, reminiscent of the sound of the body falling from the chandelier only minutes earlier.

The ghastly presence moved toward her and for the first time, Amy noticed that she was holding a very familiar doll under her arm. That same doll that she demanded Hank throw out. That same doll that the landlord Bernice had come to collect at such an odd hour, with no explanation. Amy's mind raced yet again, trying to put together all of the connections, trying to piece together a puzzle which she knew she was being shown the pieces too.

"You can't save Matilda! You can't save any of us!" the ghost screamed at Amy as it flew toward her, its face barely an inch from her own.

Amy closed her eyes tightly and prepared for the worst. Nothing happened. She sat for several minutes next to the corpse on the floor before she opened her eyes and in terror remembered where she was. The face of a rotted and maggot eaten corpse stared at her from mere feet away. Still, she was able to tell it was an Asian man. "How odd," she thought aloud.

Amy got up off of the floor, determined to figure out what it was that was happening. She began to feel heavy headed and groggy and as she approached the stairwell she collapsed, blacking out. As she plummeted down the stairs she fell into total darkness.

Amy awoke with a start, sitting up slowly and deliberately. Her head was pounding and it made her dizzy. She was sweating profusely. She found herself back in her own bedroom, next to Hank, who was still snoring loudly. She climbed out of bed and went to the kitchen to get some water.

This time going through the living room on the way. She noticed Jared there on the couch, snoring deeply himself. She was partially relieved, partially terrified. She did not know if she was awake or asleep. Amy was certain she was awake before, but it had been the most stressful day of her life and she knew her mind was quite capable of playing tricks on her. As she got into the kitchen and got her favorite mug out of the cabinet she decided to have a quick cup of water but to also make a pot of coffee. She'd have a cup and then there would be a fresh pot for Hank and Jared to enjoy in the morning.

As the coffee brewed she grew impatient with the pot. Mr. Coffee had always been too slow for her. She lit a cigarette and took a deep drag. And then it happened again. A loud thump. A sharp thud and then the house shook. Like it got hit by a wrecking ball. Amy couldn't believe that Hank and Jared were sleeping through the commotion. This time it came from the basement and not the attic.

"I don't give a damn what it is this time," Amy said out loud to the house as if it could hear her. For all she knew it could. She then took her cigarette and a cup of fresh black coffee outside with her and watched the sunrise from her front porch.

8

THE HUNTER AND THE BEAST

*A*fter Hank returned home from the hospital he found that his seizures became much more regular and severe. His quality of life was deteriorating quickly and his mental health was all but a shattered glass on the floor of sanity after his vision of Sheridan and Matilda, the rebel soldiers and The Beast; which was the term he came to adopt for that horrible nightmare that he had encountered both within his own mind and that first night in Gravel Switch...those eyes in the barn...it had to be the same thing.

His relationship with Amy seemed to be growing rockier by the day. They never had any fun together anymore and they had drifted apart quite a bit emotionally, but on some strange, unspoken level they were more dedicated to each other than ever. Hank prided himself on that even though he never discussed it with Amy. His marijuana growing and his glass-blowing were all he was focusing his time on. Amy seemed to work fifty to sixty hours a week at Walgreens and Hank mostly had the house to himself. Because of this he often invited some of the locals over to hang out with him, which they were glad to do because he kept them stoned on the best cannabis around. The real reason for Hank was just to have company with him in case he had a severe seizure and hit his head or bit his tongue. He had chipped some teeth the night he went to the hospital and he didn't want to bite his tongue off.

One such friend that would regularly visit Hank during those long days was Alan Fox. He had grown up in Gravel Switch but he lived just down the road in Bradfordsville. It was only a few mile drive for him to come visit and he and Hank spent much of the late summer and fall together becoming fast friends. Alan was nowhere near as intelligent as Hank when it came to book-smarts, which wasn't saying much since Hank was a tenth-grade dropout, but Alan had a level of awareness about country living that he was eager to learn from. He was a little taller than Hank was, about five foot ten and he had sandy blond hair that always appeared to be greasy and dirty at the same time. He had the face of a weasel and his two front teeth on both top were stacked one right behind the other making his mouth appear to be almost a snout, accentuating the already pointy features of his nose and high cheekbones. Alan always wore the same camouflage hat and often wore a camo shirt as well. He was a third-generation tobacco farmer and marijuana grower, though he raised chickens and goats and grew corn in one of his fields. Hank liked Alan's relaxed view of the world and was inspired by him to carve some of the complexity out of his own life. After all, he had moved to Gravel Switch just for that. Just to relax.

He took Hank bow hunting a few times, but it soon became obvious that Hank was too loud, too concerned with smoking weed instead of hunting and when he did manage to get a shot off...well, he was no marksman. Still, Hank was enthusiastic and would always help Alan field dress his kills and haul the meat back to the dark blue cargo van that was Alan's favorite hunting vehicle. They both ate well that fall. Lots of venison sausage, which kept their grocery bills down quite a bit.

After deer season was over and Hank had built a strong level of trust with Alan he took the local man upstairs and showed him the grow room. Alan was a cannabis grower himself, but he did an outdoor crop. He had never seen such a beautiful sight as Hank's gorgeous, well cared for, high grade indoor. He stood with his jaw slack and open just staring. "I'm impressed as hail buoy!" he eventually stated in his thick country accent that was sometimes a little much even for Hank to fully understand.

"Thanks. It's been my life's work to do this. Been working on this strain forever now, but everyone tells me it is the best shit they ever had," Hank said with obvious pride. It was one thing to get a compliment about his weed. It was another thing entirely to get a compliment from another grower, especially one that he looked up to.

Over the course of the day, Hank and Alan bonded over growing cannabis, smoking cannabis and talking about cannabis. Eventually, Hank had a seizure, but it wasn't too bad. It lasted all of a minute and he was for the most part back in control of his mental faculties quickly. Alan had never seen anyone have a seizure before, but Hank had warned him about them and Alan knew what to expect. Still, after Alan had seen him in such a compromised state and didn't seem to look at Hank any differently Hank found a new level of comfort with Alan and their friendship. Mostly because Alan didn't seem to show any sign of looking down on Hank about it, or perceiving the epilepsy as a weakness. Still, even though Alan didn't show Hank the level of concern that Amy might have shown him,

Hank was glad to have Alan there as he recovered. Unlike most of his seizures at that time, it was unaccompanied by any sort of out of body experience, vision or hallucination. Hank wasn't really sure where it was he was going when he had his worst episodes, but he was intent to keep a journal of what he was experiencing…especially because he had seen those red eyes in his barn that first night. He decided to ask Alan about them.

"Hey Alan, you ever see anything out here that has huge red eyes? And I mean huge. And they sorta glow bright, especially in the moonlight," he asked shyly, expecting that he'd be met with a mix of ignorance and rejection on the subject, but he couldn't have been more wrong.

Alan almost came out of his seat he was so shocked. Hank immediately knew he had hit a nerve. Alan cleared his throat, took a long swig off of a bottle of water that was sitting in front of him, then took a deep drag off of the joint they were sharing. He put his right index finger up to indicate that he needed a second but had an answer.

"Hank, you saw them red eyes…buoy you in danger. They been seen around here for over a hundred years, probly more'n that. They always come 'round before death. They're a local legend down here, the older folks swear they're real. I will admit that I seen 'em myself once, back in the day…" Alan trailed off and became distant and morose.

Oblivious to Alan's emotional state Hank glibly asked, "Anything happen? You said they always come with death?"

Alan sobered up quickly, Hank's voice jarring him out of the trance he was falling into. "Yeah. I seen 'em eyes out in a field, I was drivin' back from Danville, comin' home with dinner and they was just starin' at me. I stopped and got my gun off the rack and spotted down my scope. What I saw wudn't nuthin' like nuthin' I ever saw. I didn't even shoot at it, even though I done know'd the farmer whose field it was and he wouldn't mind none. I was just scare't, scare't shitless buoy. I got in my truck and that fuckin' thang was chasin' my ass. I hit a tree and totaled my truck. Spent a week in the hospital… that's why my face is like 'is," he motioned at his jaw, which until then Hank had assumed was just the mutated result of generations of inbreeding, but in that moment could easily see it had been smashed.

"Some local legends…well…they ain't just legends. Know what I'm sayin'?" Alan continued. Hank stared, transfixed by the tale. "There's weirder shit out here in 'ese woods'n you could imagine buoy!" Alan changed the mood, busting into hysterical laughter. Hank joined him, more out of discomfort than mirth.

Over the course of the next hour, they smoked a couple more joints and shared their descriptions of the physical form of The Beast. The conversation would often jar things in Alan's memory from childhood, things he'd heard about The Beast. It was much to Hank's chagrin when Alan informed him that there was not one but several of the accursed things, that they all did not look exactly alike and that they must be appeased. Alan seemed as shocked to remember these tales as Hank was to hear them. When Alan revealed the source of the fanciful stories as his great aunt, the local historian, Hank immediately knew it was Phyllis, the woman Amy had met. The woman who had warned them to leave the house. For some reason, he didn't mention his familiarity with Phyllis' stories to Alan but kept a mental note that they were kinfolk.

It dawned on Hank that everyone in the small community, hell everyone in the county, probably knew each other or knew of each other's families. He hadn't grown up in a small town and as such didn't quite understand what it was like. Making a mental leap that was a bit unusual for him when he was so thoroughly stoned Hank began to realize that if your aunt is thought of as the crazy old lady to be avoided then you probably didn't go around advertising your kinship.

"Hank, if them thangs don't eat...well, son...there's hell to be paid around 'ese parts," Alan reiterated to Hank in his slack-jawed lackadaisical way. Too stoned to know he had already gotten Hank's paranoia up with a similar statement earlier.

"Anyone ever kill one?" Hank thought he'd ask with the hope of getting to hunt something that could hunt them back. He felt his adrenaline surge a bit as he asked.

"You can't kill death itself man. Them thangs ain't of this world. They can walk through walls, come through dimensions or something. They say its fear that calls 'em here. I dunno myself. I do know I was attacked once, in the creek not half a mile from here. Had two dogs with me, coonhounds too. They would've noticed anythang with them snouts they got on 'em. Still, something jumped off the creek bank onto my back and tore me up from behind; somethin' fierce. I's knocked out, but when I come to one of my dogs was ripped to pieces. And I mean, literally. Two of its legs tore right off, thrown down the creek a ways," Alan had to stop and collect himself, the memories obviously stirring up horrible emotions that brought him into conflict with his own rational mind.

"The other dog?" Hank asked meekly and at a lowered volume, scared to offend Alan in his distressed emotional state.

"Never did find it," Alan said under his breath in a low voice, choking back what Hank knew were tears. He knew Alan was a redneck country boy and damn sure wouldn't want another man to see him cry, so he stood up and walked into the kitchen and got them both a soda. It gave Alan time to collect himself and restore his macho front. As he got the Pepsis out of the refrigerator Hank knew that he was starting to understand the country mentality.

"Well, I've seen one in my barn, the first night after I moved in. It stood there staring at me, and well… Hell yeah, I was afraid! Every time I moved it mirrored me. I panicked and ran inside. But then I had this dream, or at least I think it was a dream. Honestly, it was as real as sitting here with you right now, but then I woke up in the hospital after it was over. They said I had the worst seizure I ever had, but it seemed so damn real to me. Not like where my mind goes when I seize," Hank rambled on and on, but Alan was used to it. People out in the country had a way with stories and Hank took to that tradition quite well.

"Anyway, in this dream or vision or whatever it was…a nightmare? I dunno, but I saw the thing again. It had the same eyes. Them red eyes. But I saw the whole thing. It was like some sort of goat thing or something. It had features from all sorts of different creatures and made the most horrible noises I ever heard in my life. It had two tails and thick fur. Razor sharp claws as long as butcher's knives and they folded back like a straight razor. Its head was hideous. A horse, a ram, a jackrabbit? I dunno, maybe all of them. It couldn't be stopped, it couldn't be hurt and it couldn't be killed except when it was shot right in the eye. It just fucked up a bunch of soldiers and left as the house… This house! Or at least what it used to be like, burnt down."

"Hank that is not good. If you seen it, well…probably it seen you too. If it is coming to you, even in dreams, you need to appease it. If it don't feed, it will take you or someone you love from you. Leave it an offering. Seriously. Raw steaks, chicken. I know they love goats. Granny used to put a goat out for it every spring and it always seemed to leave us alone. She'd just put the meat on the threshold. The next day it would be gone and granny would say we was safe for the time being. Then she'd just put a big ole doormat over 'em blood stains, nobody would know nuthin'," Alan rambled on too, half to let Hank know it was alright, but half because he was stoned and liked to talk.

"Yeah, I'll do just that," Hank said, but even as he did so he thought that it all sounded too crazy. Leaving out meat or animal sacrifices to keep some sort of mythical creature at bay seemed silly and superstitious. He laughed to himself and thought, "I guess country life really is way different after all."

9

THE MONSTER AND THE MEDICINE

$\mathcal{A}$ s the summer gave way to fall the fall gave way to one of the harshest winters in as long as anyone in Gravel Switch could remember. There were days when it was so cold that Hank and Amy shut off the entire house and huddled in the master bedroom, off of the living room which they had turned into a den. It was where they gathered to smoke marijuana and listen to music, where they entertained friends anyway. It also had a set of mahogany double doors to seal it off from the living room and the rest of the house, with only the front windows and the door to the foyer letting in any of the wretched cold. With some thick plastic sheeting and a few tapestries and blankets they were able to keep the room comfortable with just a kerosene heater through the worst of it, even the ice storm that nearly destroyed Marion County that January.

On one of the coldest days of the ice storm, Amy bundled up in her pajamas and bathrobe and put on her pink bunny slippers for the arduous trip to the kitchen. As she walked down the hallway toward the back of the house she felt a strange and irresistible compulsion to go to her old bedroom. The room where she had made love to Jared. The room where, unbeknownst to her, Quan had used Yuri's body to rape Ana Sophia. As Amy entered the frigid room she could see her breath. It seemed to hang in the air as she shivered. She sat on the bed and sighed. She sat there in the cold for a long while. Hank wouldn't even seem to notice with the state he had been in. Amy knew it was getting bad, that it might be a situation where she had to dedicate the entirety of her life to taking care of a gimp who was incapable of pleasuring her. Not in the ways she wanted to be pleasured.

Amy just wanted a moment to soak in all of the mental and emotional baggage that she carried with her at all times, but seldom directly addressed for fear of having a total breakdown. As she got up to finally make her way into the kitchen she stepped on something which immediately made her jump in pain and hop on one foot. Looking down she saw that it was the bottle of pills which Jared had given to Ana Sophia when Yuri hurt his knee. She picked up the large bottle, which looked to contain a couple of hundred pills, and smiled a deep smile. This would help her get through her hard times and would keep her numb while she dealt with the horrible deaths of her friends.

Amy popped two of the opioid painkillers upon getting to the kitchen before she had even poured herself a glass of water. She pulled a bottle of Woodford Reserve, fine Kentucky bourbon, out of her cupboard and took a long pull off of it before pouring herself a hefty glass. "Fuck water," she thought. "Whiskey is all I need right about now."

Amy didn't leave the kitchen until she was well liquored up. By then, with little else on her stomach, she was starting to feel a little buzz from the pills she had eaten. She got back to the master bedroom and saw that Hank was rolling a joint. She pulled the gargantuan bottle of painkillers out of the pocket of her robe and shook them. Hank turned with a startled look on his face.

"Where did you get those?" he asked her, eyes gleaming with avarice. He rubbed his hands together, making fun of himself as he knew how he had sounded.

"These are the pills that Jared gave Ana Sophia that night of the party; when you had your worst seizure ever and they... well they..." Amy's voice trailed off, she couldn't finish her sentence, but she knew that Hank understood.

"Hell yeah, give me some!"

Amy poured a few into Hank's palm and he popped them into his mouth immediately. Now it was his turn to make the icy walk to the kitchen. Hank always had a hard time swallowing pills without anything to drink. He asked Amy for a sip off of her cup but it was whiskey and he couldn't have alcohol with his seizure medication.

That was the first day they spent with that bottle of pills and over the course of the winter, they would eat them all. By the time the first day of spring had come Amy was fully addicted to opiates. Hank had taken far less of the pills because he already took so many Valium and with his other seizure medications, he didn't want to overdo it. Still, with all the pills he did manage to eat and all the time he stayed completely intoxicated Hank didn't notice at all that his wife became a junkie right before his eyes.

Amy began to steal things from the stock room at work.

There were always returns and exchanges that got lost in the system. There were items which went on clearance and then got returned to the warehouse. Then there were items which she marked down with her managerial abilities, which with her employee discount became basically free. Hank started getting on her by mid-spring about how many things she was bringing home. Everything from toothbrushes to lawn chairs. From boxes of candy to charcoal grills. She even brought home inflatable pool toys although they did not have a pool. Hank was annoyed, but he was hoarding almost as much as she was. With his income from his grow operation he was making ten thousand dollars a month, which was more than he was easily able to spend, isolated as he was. Deep in the bowels of Marion County Kentucky. With so much more money than he had ever been used to having Hank bought all of the toys he had wanted when he was a kid but his parents couldn't afford. At first, he was dismayed to see how expensive they were, but he soon got over that. He was just excited that with the internet and auction websites every toy he had ever had or wanted and many he never even knew existed were available at the click of a button. He spent thousands of dollars on Star Wars toys from the nine-teen seventies and eighties. He bought Robotech toys which were rare in Kentucky when he grew up. He bought Trans-formers and G.I. Joe men. For Amy he found her favorite dolls; Strawberry Shortcake and all of her friends. She was legiti-mately shocked to get them and displayed them prominently throughout the house.

Eventually, as spring wore on Hank was on a good track to make good on the ten thousand clones that the Cornbread Mafia were demanding in payment for disappearing the bodies of Yuri and his wife. He was doing well financially and Amy got a promotion at her job. Everything was going well for them, although there wasn't much intimacy left in their marriage. Hank didn't seem to mind or notice at all, but when Amy brought it up he would always apologize profusely and pleasure her as best he could. When he was unable to get it up, which was more often the case than not, he would pleasure her orally. So when Hank took all things into consideration he thought of his life and their life together as pretty sweet for the most part. Sure they had their ups and downs but mostly life had been good for them. So Hank decided to ask Amy about expanding their family.

"Amy, our family is too small. We need to bring in another member. Somebody to love us unconditionally. Somebody to always be there for us and with us, somebody for us to always be there for too," Hank felt awkward talking about this subject out of the blue but decided that was the best approach. To take her off guard a bit and gauge her initial response.

"Hank, you always said you didn't want kids. You have said since day one that you don't want to pass on your genes because your dad was epileptic. Because you are epileptic and you don't want your kid to suffer from that too. What made you change your mind?" she seemed outright shocked, not only that he brought the subject of kids up, but in the way he had done it. From out of nowhere.

"What? No, no, no. You have me all wrong Amy. I want to get a dog!" he was emphatic and animated for somebody who had eaten so many Valium that morning.

They shared a good laugh and then they did just that. They went to the pound and got a dog. He was a shy, bashful, under-sized and malnourished looking pit bull with white fur with black and brown splotches all over. He was all wiggles as soon as they saw him and they both knew in that instant that he would be their dog, despite having not looked through all of the dogs at the pound.

When they got him out of his cage he was all love and affection. They noticed some scarring on his head and legs and the shelter informed them that he had been a fighting dog. He obviously wasn't very successful and had been turned loose by his owner. They didn't have a name on file for him so Amy named him Boris after Boris and Natasha from The Bullwinkle Show. Within half a day of getting him home it was more than obvious that Boris liked Hank, but he was Amy's dog. He loved her unconditionally and guarded her loyally and fiercely. With Boris the duo became a trio and the dog quickly assumed his role as the third member of the family.

With the changing of the seasons Hank's seizures became much more severe and common. He had Jared come over and prescribe him a more potent seizure medication, but first, he had to wean off of his old medication. This proved incredibly hard for Hank, but by the end of spring he made the switch and was getting some sense of relief. His seizures went from several a day, sometimes a dozen, to several a week. Jared upped his dosage on Valium, prescribed him muscle relaxers and gave him a Vicodin prescription as well so that in case he ever needed them he had them. Hank was grateful.

Jared also gave Amy a new prescription for painkillers after she explained to him that she had found Ana Sophia's bottle and taken them all over the last few months. He did not scold her as she thought he would and wrote her a prescription with a higher dosage and unlimited refills. She was shocked and thankful. She was just at the state where she understood that she was addicted and was relieved that she would be able to quit on her own terms. She wouldn't have to buy on the black market, beg, borrow or steal to get her fix. She simply had to go to the pharmacy, literally at Walgreens where she worked, and could fill her prescription at any time.

One night in early April after a long day at Walgreens, on her feet, dealing with attitudinal customers, Amy headed home with a mind thick and cloudy from all the pills she had been popping throughout the day. When she got about a hundred yards from her own driveway something appeared on the road in front of her. Something too big to just run over. Before she could discern whether it was a horse or a deer or what it was she had swerved and wrecked into a guardrail.

When she came to her hood was up and the engine pouring smoke. At least she only had a few feet to walk to her driveway, but the driveway itself was nearly a quarter mile long. She sighed, turned on the hazard lights and grabbed her flashlight out of the glove box. The wind was a bit cold so she tightened her hood up around her head. She bent into the wind and clutched her hooded sweatshirt closed as she made her way towards her house.

She got to her driveway soon enough and she could easily see the lights on in her house. It wouldn't be long until she would be inside, with Hank, warming herself. She tried to reach him on her cell phone, but he didn't answer.

Hank awoke the next morning to find Amy face down on the front porch. Her clothes were shredded off of her back and she had several slices from right shoulder to left hip. She had obviously lost a lot of blood, but when he opened the door she let out a moan that let him know she was still alive.

"Oh, fuck!" Hank screamed aloud as he ran back inside, going immediately for his cordless phone, fingers frantically pressing 9-1-1. Before he could hit the dial button Amy called out to him from the porch in a voice strained with extreme pain.

"Hank, don't call the ambulance. Don't! Remember the party…call Jared. Call Jared. Call Jar…" her voice trailed off as she lost consciousness.

Hank erased the numbers he had put into the phone and looked Jared up by name on the handset. He hit dial and crossed his fingers, running back out to the porch to Amy's side, praying to the god he did not believe in.

10

THE THING IN THE BASEMENT

*A*my's recovery proved to be long and arduous. She had five lacerations across the entirety of her torso, from shoulder to hip. They were deep gashes that the doctors were baffled by. The only common ground that any of the professionals who looked after her during her hospitalization could agree upon was that it was some sort of animal which had attacked her. The wounds were incredibly slow to heal and remained infected for over a month despite a hardcore regimen of antibiotics. Amy knew she would no longer be comfortable wearing the backless patchwork shirts that she was so fond of sporting in the summer time. It was a status symbol among hippie girls to have high quality, handmade clothing and Amy had spent quite a bit of money on patchwork shirts. She had invested years into cultivating her look and it was depressing for her to know that she would have to come up with a new style or leave her hideous scars exposed to the world.

Hank came out to Lexington, to the University of

Kentucky hospital, as often as he could to see his wife as she recovered. With his epilepsy, it wasn't safe for him to drive, although he did so a few times and lied to Amy as to how he had come to town. Thankfully since Jared worked at UK hospital Hank was often able to catch a ride with him, both to and from seeing Amy. Hank was happy that Jared was there for them like he was. If it weren't for Jared they would both have a hard time getting the medications they needed. Hank's new seizure medication was working much better than the last stuff he was taking. He had a never-ending supply of Valium and Vicodin and he stayed pretty much too mellow for stress to trigger seizures like they did before. Although he still had them they didn't dominate his life like they once had. Because of this, Hank did not notice the monkey on his back. He was unaware that the cold fingers of addiction were gripped about his throat. He could still breathe but should have been feeling that grip tighten. With his mind on Amy and her recovery at pretty much all times that shadow easily crept in and blotted out what light he had in his life.

Those spring and summer days alone in the house proved to take quite a toll on Hank's mental health. He didn't feel a disconnect like he did with his addiction. He knew he was going slowly crazy. On some levels, he embraced it. That his mind was shattered beyond repair was the one thing on which he could rely. How else could the beasts in the woods be explained? How else could the whispers he heard all throughout his house be explained? The doll, the dreams, the visions during his seizures. None of it made sense to Hank, that is unless he was suffering from an overwhelming madness.

So he wore that label like a mantle, made it his armor. His craziness would be the anchor to his sanity. Some days Hank would awaken into the house and was sure it was the nine-teenth century again. Other days he would see a little girl in a white dress playing in the living room or the front yard. Always she carried a doll with her and over time Hank came to believe he was seeing the very same doll that he had found in his attic and thrown out. That creepy doll from the wheelchair, that Bernice had just mysteriously known had been found. "Did she really show up the next morning to take it back, without any possible way of knowing they had found it? "

A man whose sanity was questionable was an easier way for Hank to identify than as a man who was experiencing extreme situations and supernatural events. Still, even if it was just in his mind he lived in terror for the most part. Through that terror, and the anxiety it brought with it, Hank's mental faculties deteriorated to a wretched state of paranoia. Every creak and moan the old house made was a nightmare come to life, a sword forged in the crucible of his imagination whose blade carved easily through his shattered mind.

The days would come and go and sometimes Hank did not even notice. Between cowering through his own fear and over-medicating with his prescriptions he did little living; he simply existed. Without Amy in the house, all he had to talk to were Boris and the ghosts of the past occupants, the ghosts in which he held no belief. Boris did not seem to have any inclination toward bonding with Hank but wasn't unnecessarily cold to him either. As he waited on his momma to return from the hospital he tolerated Hank and was not shy in the least about letting him know when it was time for food, or to go outside to use the bathroom. The ghosts of Gravel Switch, on the other hand, did all they could to get Hank to engage with them.

From full form visual manifestations to loud bumps and

bangs in the night they constantly tried every trick they could think of to get Hank's attention. He had shown no interest at all since he began to place all the blame of what was happening on his lessening mental capabilities. Even times when he would come to direct physical harm because of their actions or pranks Hank was able to write off as his mind playing tricks on him.

Still, the day came when his lack of faith in what he was experiencing was challenged. Two nights before Amy was due to come home from the hospital after her six-week stay Hank heard a noise so strange and so unique that he had no choice but to investigate its source. Walking through the kitchen he found that it emanated from the laundry room. From the back wall, where there was an old door to the basement. As he approached Hank realized that he had not yet been in the basement. He had in fact never even opened the door. Yet that night it stood ajar a few inches. The strange noise growing slowly but steadily louder. It was such an odd sound that it seemed to be a menagerie of other noises. There was a dull long foghorn sound that was a massive white noise behind a wall of insects chattering, chitinous legs of crickets screeching alongside the undulating waves of locusts. There was thunder and heavy breathing. All these noises rolled into one cacophonous audible mass that assailed Hank's mind as much as it overwhelmed his ears.

He used his cell phone as a flashlight as he pulled the basement door open with a loud creak from rusty old hinges. Immediately he was overwhelmed with a dampness thick with mold, mildew, spores…he could not tell what all he was breathing but it had a foulness too it from, what Hank assumed to be, staying closed up and moist for decades. The noise became louder, intoxicating, drawing him ever closer even as it made his body and mind both more uncomfortable by the second. His curiosity peaking he peered into the basement, down those rickety old steps, into the darkness that his phone's light would not penetrate more than a few feet.

As his foot hit the top step and he began his descent into the unknown dark a smell foul and rotten overcame all of his senses. He spun to his left side ninety degrees and vomited involuntarily out of reflex. Whatever he had smelled hit him like a miasma of sewage and pestilence. He got woozy and stumbled down the next few steps before regaining his footing, lashing out with his right hand, clasping for the handrail. When he got to the bottom of the twelve steps he found a light switch and turned it on. The bulb reluctantly flickered on, gasping for a moment in protest as if being called upon to work were asking too much. Yet still, it was dutiful and lit the immediate area thoroughly.

Hank was shocked to see that the basement was essentially empty. There were a few old trunks and chests, an old wine shelf that was empty but otherwise the basement was empty of objects.

It was not, however, empty of things. In the corner farthest from the stairs, Hank perceived something so alien to his consciousness that he doubted that even his own schizophrenic nightmares could conceive of such a horror. It was surely the source of all the crazy noises and the wretched smells that made him puke and gag upon his own bile. Hank knew this thing was in all likelihood the source of his own insanity, of the strange and violent events that had occurred since he moved into the house. Just one second of gazing his eyes upon its hideousness and Hank knew all those things.

A foul beast that resembled a maggot the size of a small car writhed in the corner. It had a series of legs as if a centipede down each side of the lower half of it and it stood upright from what appeared to function as a waist from the upper half. The bloated and distended body was a sickening green-grey and pulsed with thick blood vessels that steadily pumped a thick black ichor throughout the repellent form. Two eyes stared down at Hank, who was only about half of its height. Eyes that seemed far too small for a thing of such proportions, similar to those of a blue whale. They looked glazed over, dead, like a blind man's eyes. Yet Hank knew that they could see everything that he was, everything he knew, everything he was made of... down to the molecular level. The bulbous mass that functioned like a head split and peeled apart vertically, revealing a maw containing row upon row of barbed hooks. It had squid-like, ropey tentacles writhing from its back, tasting the air about Hank's face as they inched toward him, dripping slimy green goo from their tips. Hank stared in absolute and abject horror with his mouth wide open. He did not know whether he stood paralyzed with fear or whether he was subdued by some strange power of the thing which clearly was physically before him.

"So, you did hear my call," a voice like icy daggers bypassed Hank's ears and entered straight into his brain. He realized that it was telepathic as it had used no mouth to produce the voice. "I can taste your fear. You will do just fine. A flavor like yours comes but once a millennia. Yes. Yessss...."

Hank's heart was racing. He could feel his pulse pounding in his neck, in his temple, in his wrists. Sweat poured down his forehead and dizziness overwhelmed him again. The sound of the beast before him had not subsided, even during its telepathic speech. He was the prey, he knew it. He had never felt like a predator but had never felt like prey either. In this moment he knew the fear of the door mouse when it meets the house cat. Trembling he braced as two of the lashing tentacles came to rest upon his face, one on each cheek. He felt suckers pulling at his face, then hooks tear into his flesh through them. He could not pull away without mutilating his face. The tentacles seemed to pulse and then Hank became aware that this thing was drinking. And what it was drinking was him! Without any other course of action coming immediately to mind, he yelled at the horror.

"Please, don't kill me! Please!" he wet himself as he yelled at the grotesque monstrosity.

"Kill you? I am eating your fear!" the voice penetrated Hank's brain in a tone intimating that he should be thanking the abomination. "You could not even begin to fathom that which I am taking from you, that which I want of you and that which I will have of you in days to come. Still, do not worry yourself, it will all be over soon."

Hank trembled and pissed himself again as he saw his life flashing before his eyes. Despite his absolute terror, he became more and more relaxed each moment. He could tell that the thing was injecting something into him to keep him calm, some juice full of a that which was a blasphemy against nature. Hank forced his eyes open to look once again upon the utter horror of the thing and noticed that the fabric of reality itself was peeling apart around it. The air swirled in vortices opening and closing portals to strange dimensions, undulating in waves of color and sound, the makeup of space-time distorting and warping around that sluggish maggot that Hank could neither describe as wholly alien nor wholly demon but as some strange amalgamation of both which should not exist. Yet it writhed before him as it fed on his essence. Yes, that is what it was taking from him. Not his blood, nor his fear as it claimed. It was sucking him dry of his very life force. Some strange, vampiric thing, from God only knew what wretched corner of the galaxy, was going to drink him away.

"You have no right!" he screamed at it. "My soul is mine and mine alone, you cannot take it. My life force is mine, you cannot have it!"

"Silly mortal, you are my plaything, whether you like it or not. Your soul has belonged to me since you stepped over the threshold into this house. I was ancient before the star which this pathetic planet orbits was born from the primordial fire. I have eaten worlds, slain gods, reaped the souls of entire galaxies. And you claim your soul for your own? So be it then mortal. If you can manage to hold onto it then it is yours. But…before I am done with you…you will give it unto me willingly. You will beg me to take it from you like the burden which it is. Otherwise, left to your own devices, you will only find oblivion."

Hank was slow to respond, though as rapidly as the thoughts of what he would say gathered in his brain the thing knew them. He could not hide from it. Every word it spoke was true, he knew that, deep in his core, in his heart and soul he knew that. When he did finally find the words to speak he noticed that the tentacles embedded in his face were no longer there, though he could not recall them receding away from him they obviously had. He touched his cheeks with hands expecting to find mutilated or punctured flesh, but instead, he was unmarred by the intrusive touch of its alien tendrils.

All of the physical structure of the basement seemed to have faded away into a congeries of chromatic sprays and strobing, floating orbs of light which pulsed and glowed in rhythm with the black ichor pumping through the maggot's physical veins. Somehow Hank understood that the lights he perceived were just as much a part of it and its consciousness as anything inside of its body. As he finally opened his mouth to speak he wondered if our physical reality was even capable of holding the entirety of the creature as he realized it existed partially in some other cosmic plane.

"I would rather have oblivion than to give myself to you willingly," Hank tried to be as defiant as possible. "Did you take the souls of all the ghosts of this house then? Is that why they are all trapped here? They belong to you, don't they? I don't want to end up like them."

"I have placed my mark upon you mortal. Know this and despair. I have laid claim to you throughout all realms and across all realities. You were given to me by my earthly follow- ers, yet I shall release you for a price," the sound of its voice came as a hoard of locusts flying through a jet engine and gave Hank an instant migraine.

Hank wondered what it meant about earthly followers, but thought it best not to ask about it and to just be as straightforward as possible. "What is the price?" he played along with it.

"Three lives. The Charlatan. The Adulteress. The Young Novice. Feed me these three lives, no more, no less. No others will do. The rituals of desecration will come naturally as I guide your hand in doing my work. Three lives for one soul. That is the deal."

Hank found that darkness was overtaking his vision. The sight of the physical aspect of the monster was gone from his view, though he still felt its presence. It was only the flickers of the tears in reality and the glowing orbs of strobing, incandes- cent contagion that remained for Hank to see, the rest swallowed up by a sea of blackness, that was covering everything like a thick ink.

"Ok," was all Hank could manage to say as total darkness overwhelmed him.

*H*ank awoke several hours later according to his watch. He was passed out on the floor in the laundry room. To his astonishment, he found that there was no basement door in the laundry room at all. Just as he thought, again, all in his head! Hank knew he was crazy. It was only a matter of time until his delusions became so realistic, he knew that. Still, he couldn't get over how intense the situation had seemed. He went into the kitchen, made a cup of coffee and called up his friend Alan, who came over immediately.

Hank recalled the events of the evening as quickly and as explicitly as he could. He was candid with Alan that he doubted his mental health, yet still, Alan could see that he was shaken and was genuinely afraid. To Hank's surprise, he was totally open to everything that Hank had to tell him. Perhaps it would have been different if they had not shared their experiences with the beasts in the woods with one another. The foundation of that bond and how Alan treated him the same as he ever did meant the world to Hank in the wake of his experience, whether it was a mental breakdown or not.

"Hank it's funny to me that you mention 'at monster. My great aunt use' to tell me stories 'bout it when I was a kid. Tried'a keep me outta his house, which me an' my friends use' to like playin' in when we was little."

Hank began to freak out a bit inside, he bit his lip a little out of stress. Then he asked Alan the one thing he wanted to know the most, "What is it, man? I mean, what the hell is it!?"

"I dunno. I never believed it was real. But if you seen it, even in a dream or a seizure…I dunno. 'at might change thangs a little," Alan showed his doubt, but not in the existence of the monster. Hank could tell by the man's body language that he was holding back.

"This wasn't either of those!" Hank interrupted out of frustration. "I was lucid and awake."

"Either way…it's just too much coincidence, cuz everything you said is what my auntie use' to tell me. Supposedly its some sort of demon. It's been in 'ese hills since before God himself was born. They say them things that's out here in 'ese woods… well them's its children. It's spawn. Supposedly some of the local folk use' to sacrifice their kids to it, back over a hundred years ago. I dunno…mostly just stories I heard. I mean I never believed 'em at all. But damn, I mean, you never even heard of it and you seen it. That's just freaky," Alan seemed genuinely scared in a way Hank had never seen before. It was more than obvious that the conversation was making him uncomfortable.

"So, what do we call it? I mean, what did y'all call it when you were kids Alan?"

"We called it the Larvamog. Cuz it's like a big ole maggot thing," Alan said, a shiver going up his spine that made him shudder as he finished the thought. "The old folks use' to say its true name was Larvothmagog or some such shit."

"He's seen it too." Hank thought to himself. Alan wasn't as good at hiding things as Hank was at picking up on them. "Let's smoke a joint and figure out what to do about this Larvamog. I know I'm crazy…but maybe I'm just picking up on the collective consciousness of the local fears. Or maybe this thing is actually real. If it is? Well, damn, it's kinda up to us to fuck that thing up if we can. To take it out," Hank was feeling powerful at the thought of making war on something, on anything. His impotence had left him feeling wholly inadequate. The thought of taking the fight to a giant, demonic space-maggot gave him an emotional surge inside that was the closest thing he had known in months to feeling virile. And whether Alan was onboard or not Hank knew in that moment that he would dedicate everything he had left to fighting that horrible, grotesque monstrosity.

"Larvamog…buoy, it's a demon supposedly. I guess we could try, but I dunno 'bout fightin' no demons," Alan was a country boy. Of course he would be superstitious, especially about local legends; still, Hank thought that Alan would be nearly as gung-ho as he was to put a big hurt on that damned abomination. Hank knew for sure that he was in it alone. Alan didn't even want to believe in it. He feared it. But he would not fight it.

After Alan had gone home Hank got a good night's sleep. He had one more day before he was to go into Lexington with Jared to pick Amy up from the hospital. She had recovered from the wounds easily enough, but contracted a nasty strain of the MERSA virus and had to be treated with experimental drugs and antibiotics. That gave Hank a solid day to build a plan. If he couldn't count on Alan's help then he probably wouldn't get anyone in Marion County to help him. Normally he would have turned to his friend Yuri in an intense situation, but he still hadn't come to terms with what happened to the Almeidas. The thought of needing his old friend there brought him no comfort and left a hole in his heart which he had to ignore in order to function at all. Hank knew he was shoving some heavy emotional weight to the back burner and he knew that eventually it would boil over and cause a mess, but in the moment he had no focus to deal with how he had been feeling.

Getting Amy home from the hospital was enough of an emotional roller coaster.

With no living person to turn to Hank decided to finally reach out to the spirits in the house who had been so adamant about getting his attention. He didn't know how to do it, but he knew that after the way Alan had acted that he wasn't crazy, or at least not delusional. Nobody could have normal mental health after seeing Larvamog. Whether flesh and blood, or hallucination, or both, it was madness itself just to gaze upon the cursed thing. So he postulated that if he could believe in giant space-maggots then he could believe in ghosts. Especially with all of the shit they had pulled on him. The bumps in the night, the little girl with the white dress and the creepy toy doll, furniture rearranging itself, that was just the beginning of the insanity he had been dealing with. He couldn't believe how dismissive he had been of his own experiences. Still, it had been a mechanism to try to maintain his sanity, just as then in that moment embracing it became. It was a sort of cognitive dissonance that Hank was eager to engage in, though he did see the contradiction.

"Whatever it takes to get this shit out of my life," Hank said to himself as a mantra, repeating it every twenty minutes or so.

Hank spent the rest of the day on the internet researching demons and their weaknesses, extraterrestrials and how to contact ghosts. He read articles and websites all day long, through the evening, only leaving the computer to eat and use the bathroom and to make Boris dinner and let him out. The fight had become his new obsession.

"I will save myself. I will save Amy. I will save the whole damn town, but most of all I will save the tormented souls that were helplessly trapped in this damn house!" Hank felt alive at the sound of his voice roaring through the house as Boris stared at him, barking in excitement.

Even though Hank was sitting at his computer desk and reading he envisioned himself as a knight of righteousness, taking up arms in the fight against a cosmic evil which only he had the power to defeat. Hell, only he was truly aware of it. Still, one thought persisted that caused him much consternation and doubt, "If it is a larva then what does it turn into?"

11

THE RAILWAYMAN

*a*my came home from the hospital to find the house was a total mess, but she didn't care. She was just happy to be home with Boris and, to a lesser extent, with Hank. She had Jared write her new prescriptions and they called them in, to the Walgreen's she worked at, and picked them up on the way home.

Amy was thankful that Jared had been there for her, but had seen quite enough of him while she was in the hospital. As much as she loved being with him, near him, talking to him, even fucking him, she had begun to fear him. And Amy knew it was all in her own head and she shouldn't hold it against him, but she had experienced several nightmares featuring him while she was in the hospital. The kind of nightmares from which she would wake up screaming and wake up all of the other patients on the floor. As Amy thought on it she realized that she had only dreamt nightmares while in the hospital. Not necessarily all bad dreams about Jared, but all bad dreams nonetheless.

Sleeping in her own bed would be a good reprieve from

that bed of terrors that she had known for the past six weeks. Hank had Alan bring over a bucket of Kentucky Fried Chicken extra crispy with all the sides and extra biscuits. It was her favorite fast food and she looked forward to chowing down on that greasy, heavenly goodness. Hospital food was always appalling to Amy, but six weeks of it was much more than she could bear. With Hank's income from his weed growing she was used to eating steak, lobster, pork chops, casseroles, scallops, and clams, whatever she wanted. Most of what she found palatable in the hospital had been brightly colored gelatinous dishes, not all of which were necessarily Jell-O.

Hank was surprisingly quiet on the ride home and Amy wondered if he was aware that she had been with Jared. She didn't really care, she knew that he would have to understand or their marriage would end. Either way, Amy had made peace with the possibility. She knew that she deserved happiness, especially after all that had happened. Guilt-free happiness was exactly what she wanted. After all of those weeks in the hospital, Amy asked Jared if she should leave Hank and if he would be interested in being with her. To her absolute astonishment, Jared suggested that she try to work it out with Hank and promised to prescribe Hank something for erectile dysfunction.

And that was where things were for her. On the edge of falling apart, riding on uncertainty. Amy's only option was to just let it play out and see what happened. So in light of that, she was simply all good with whatever happened. In fact, she looked forward to some major change, just anything but life as usual.

When they got back to their place Hank made a pot of coffee and they smoked a few bowls from Hank's favorite pipe with Jared. It wasn't long before they were all good and stoned and Jared had to be off to feed his pets. As soon as he left Hank began to tell Amy about all of the events that occurred while she was healing and everything that had happened in the house or on the property that he had yet to tell her about. He talked for hours and she barely responded at all, just a few nods and, "uh huh's."

When he was done Amy took a few deep breaths, which put Hank on edge immediately. He became in an instant paranoid, unable to resist falling into the pit of despair that came with it. Yet when she spoke it was everything Hank wanted to hear.

"I believe everything that you say, Hank. Everything. I'm just glad that you recognize now that you aren't crazy. Or aren't just crazy," she laughed. "I have had a lot of things I have experienced too and I will tell you about them all. But first I need to tell you about that night," Amy shuddered as she spoke. "Whatever attacked me, it was some sort of red-eyed monster from hell or something. It was just like what you said you saw, baby. It was something altogether unnatural. I was so afraid. But it spoke to me. It spoke! It said that it wasn't going to kill me, not yet at least. But it made damn sure to let me know that it, or they if there's more than one like you say, wasn't after me. They are after you, Hank. I don't know why, but they want to scare you, hurt you, kill you. They want to eat your fucking soul Hank and I am caught in the middle! We need to move the fuck out of here. Now."

"Amy we can't. I have to get five thousand more clones to Jared's friends," Hank lied to her so she didn't worry. He had been late on his first round of cuttings, the clones that would be the next multi-ton harvest of central Kentucky outdoor. He had actually only been able to come through with two thousand. He had no idea what the repercussions would be but he knew he would be punished somehow. He knew that as the season wore on there would be little time left to plant. He popped a couple of Valium so that he could calm down a bit, worried that he would have a seizure on Amy's first night home.

"Goddamn it! Fuck!" Amy became exasperated. "I forgot all about that. I can try to talk to Jared, to see if we can work something out. Fuck!"

"Yeah, we can't go anywhere. Where else are we gonna be able to grow thousands of clones? I took everything off of the mother plant too. I cut all I could without putting her into shock and killing her. There aren't five more clones to cut, let alone five thousand. We are pretty much fucked. I mean if they can do what they did with the Almeidas then what will and what can they do to us?" Hank began to tremble as he spoke. Nothing had prepared him for the house, but at least he knew Amy was on his side. She would be there with him to fight the demons of the house. And hell, if they prevailed then they could live in that big, beautiful house in peace and quiet. Just as they had dreamed of what seemed to be a thousand years ago.

They held each other on the couch for an hour or so after their long talk. Boris cuddled up on the cushion next to Amy and slept next to her, snoring obnoxiously. Hank felt much stronger with Amy there. The three of them, as a family, were a much more significant spiritual force than he was alone. He finally felt capable of defeating the monster now that Amy was with him again. He imagined her as a Valkyrie, wielding light and righteousness against that foul cosmic horror whose image he could not unsee, nor whose maddening wrenching of reality he could not un-know. Yes, his team was coming together.

She fell into a deep sleep on the couch in his arms. He held her for a long while and eventually shook her awake and marched her and Boris off to bed. They had moved their bedroom back into the smaller room down the hall after winter was over and turned the master bedroom into an extension of the living room, more of a den than anything else. After he got Amy to bed he went into the kitchen and made himself a cup of coffee.

It was going to be a long night for Hank, he had much more research to do. It was Amy's first night home, so he had decided to let her off the hook, but in the morning he planned on confronting her about Jared. He was sure there was something going on with the two of them. He didn't care if they were having an affair, as long as Amy was honest with him about it. Hank kind of felt okay with the idea of her receiving sexual pleasure from someone else as he was beginning to realize that he knew he had really let her down. Still, he would try in the morning to make love to his wife. Jared had slipped him a couple of Viagra on the way out the door in a move which surprised Hank to his core. He had tried not to show his shock as he took them, cooly.

After Hank got his coffee he packed the bowl of his pipe and stopped by the bedroom to kiss Amy on the forehead. He made his way to the computer and sat down intending to spend the entirety of the night researching paranormal events as he had done the night before. It was after several hours of churning through website after website that he finally found what he was most looking for. An ancient tome from an obscure library in Bulgaria had an account of something quite like Larvothmagog. A soul-eating demon that came in the form of a maggot-like abomination. The text was little and what was there seemed too vague to glean much from, but Hank did learn one clue with which he hoped to find others. The foul beast was not a singularity unto itself, but just one of a foul race of nightmares which predated humanity itself. More than one cult throughout recorded history had worshipped them and most accounts seemed to refer to them simply as the Great Old Ones.

"That seems like enough information to go looking for more," Hank said aloud to himself before pulling a long deep hit off of his pipe. "It will probably be much easier to find out about these things in general than just Larvamog specifically," as Hank spoke aloud he realized that he was speaking to himself and was shocked to find that he was much more comfortable with that than he thought he would be.

Realizing what he had accomplished Hank decided to retire to bed. It wasn't long before he needed to be up anyway and some time next to Amy, just feeling her warmth, would be good for him. Sleep found him quickly and easily. He fell straight into a dark dream, again in the house but again in the nineteenth century. It was a bright sunny day, yet everything seemed dark and gloomy. He saw the little girl with the white dress playing in the hallway, playing with her doll. Matilda. But the doll appeared to be brand new. Hank finally got a good look at her face and noticed that she was cute as a button, dark-skinned, with a mix of Asian and African features.

She disappeared as soon as he got a good look at her, but he was quite aware that she had seen him too. Perhaps he scared her? He walked out onto the front porch and was surprised to see a middle-aged Asian man sitting in a rocking chair, whittling on a piece of wood with a moonshine jug sitting at his feet and a long blade of straw in his mouth.

"Have a seat, Hank," the man knew who he was. "We need to talk."

"Who are you?" Hank asked, clueless to the man's identity.

"I'm Quan Fong. I lived here from 1893 to 1905. I actually built the house as you see it, as it stands today. On the foundation of the original house, the one that burnt down," he went on with a thick accent, both Asian and hillbilly.

"Oh," was all Hank could manage.

"So, you know 'bout the fire. Ok. Thing is Hank, that maggot…it wants somethin' from you. It wants you to do somethin' for it. But I intend to stop you. What it wants from you… well it won't deliver on its promise back in return. It cannot be trusted. Unless you leave here, never come back….it will have your soul. And trust me, I know all 'bout that. It has mine. This house is my prison and I cannot leave this land. Not so long as that thing lives and I don't 'spect it to die anytime soon. It is older than the world itself," Quan spoke to Hank deliberately, making sure he absorbed every word.

"Can we join together to fight it? Me and you, any others too?"

"I thought you would never ask," Quan replied, laughing a bit to himself. "I don't have even my soul to give, but whatever there is of me that I got left I will use it to help you. I don't want to wait 'til eternity ends to get revenge."

"How about Sheridan?" Hank remembered the man with the torch, who had set the house on fire back during the civil war.

"He cannot be trusted. He is the thrall of the maggot. Sheridan, that poor soul. He lost it all just as I did. This house took everything from him," the voice of Quan trailed off into nothingness as darkness overwhelmed Hank. He awoke in his bed next to Amy, sweating profusely and shaking.

When he awoke she was already up, doing some dishes in the kitchen. "Amy, I had the strangest dream. I met a ghost on the front porch who knew about what we are facing," he began his story as he entered the kitchen, wiping sleep out of his eyes.

"What are Great Old Ones, Hank?" she interrupted. "I had

really weird dreams too. Well, nightmares really. It just doesn't stop, does it? Asleep or awake, living in this house is some sorta hellish nightmare."

Hank recalled all he had learned the night before and Amy listened intently. By the time he was done speaking he had forgotten all about his plans for her that morning. When it dawned on him later that afternoon that he still needed to confront her about Jared the stress built up inside of him and unleashed itself as a massive seizure which left him in a daze for much of the rest of the day. Amy took care of him as best she could but was aware of the resentment growing inside of her. She wanted to be happy, not to spend her life taking care of Hank. In that moment she realized that she truly loved him if she was willing to give up all of her own dreams and ambitions to stay by his side watching him suffer.

12

THE BOOK AND THE FIRE

*a*fter several days of talking over what to do about their situation, Hank and Amy Ramsey decided that they needed outside help, in any form they could get. After hours of deliberation on who to go to, even for advice, they settled on paying Phyllis a visit. Although Hank was aware that Phyllis was the great aunt of Alan and Alan for sure knew more than he was saying Hank still trusted Amy's feelings about Phyllis.

Amy called her on the phone and Phyllis seemed to already be aware that they needed her help. Amy had to remind herself that the old woman was psychic. It was a short conversation, which Hank was thankful for as he just wanted to get there and to get answers as to what they should do about their situation.

Just as they were leaving the house and Amy was starting the car up Hank got a call on his cell phone. He was greeted by a sinister voice on the other end, dripping with coldness and venom, yet somehow Hank felt he had heard it before.

"You done fucked up buoy. We know you ain't got our clones done. We ain't the type of folks you need to be doin' that way. This is your only warning Hank. Get in touch through the usual channels and make this as right as you can. But I really don't see this one workin' out too good for ya," the voice showed no emotion at all except for malice and it scared Hank as much as any of the supernatural events which had been dominating his life and his sanity.

He simply hung up without speaking. He gave Amy a look which let her know at once that they were not in a good place with the Cornbread Mafia. He showed a stress and a pain in his face that she had seldom seen and she expected that he would soon fall into a seizure. She gave it a moment then saw that he was going to be alright. When she was certain Amy drove down the driveway, finally toward Phyllis' house and finally toward, hopefully, some sort of answers.

They arrived in only a few minutes time, it was not very far and Amy started to feel a little shame that she had only visited the old woman when something was wrong and she thought Phyllis could help. In that moment Amy felt quite a bit like a user and a fair-weather friend.

When they got out of the car they found Phyllis in the yard untying a pig which had been bound to a stake in the front yard.

"Go on now, you're free. Get outta here. Hell is on the way piggy! Go on now!" Phyllis yelled at the pig as she chased it out of the yard and into a field. She seemed to take little notice of them and then spun abruptly on her heel and looked Hank up and down quickly, leaving him feeling naked and exposed.

"Come on now dears. We have precious little time," she motioned them into her trailer. That dilapidated surf green monstrosity which of the two Ramseys only Amy had ever visited.

They entered her trailer to find it completely empty of

anything except for her dining room table and chairs. There was a large photo album on the table. She motioned for each of them to take a seat.

"Hi Phyllis. Thanks for seein' us. We really need your help. It has gotten so outta hand at our house that we just can't take it anymore," Amy was almost crying as she spoke with a hard sobbing she couldn't control.

"Amy, Hank, you are both in grave danger. I see only darkness when I look at your futures. I cannot foresee your paths, which is very rare indeed. There are dark forces working against you that I cannot comprehend. I have only heard the stories, the wive's tales and read the journals of some of the victims. But Hank you have faced that remarkable beast, that ultimate unfathomable evil. It is you who should be educating me," she laughed to let him know she was not serious.

Out of nowhere, Amy asked Phyllis, "Why did you set that pig free?"

"Oh, I won't need it any longer deary. It was just here to act as appeasement should that horror or its young ever come here, for me and mine," Phyllis smiled to reassure Amy but it did not work. "My days have come to an end. It is the burden of someone with my particular gift. We know when our own time will come."

"Damn," Hank and Amy both said in unison, mouths open, exuding sympathy for the sage old woman as much as denial and confusion at what she had said.

"Take this book. It has much of that which you want to know in it. Nothing of the maggot, but many of those it tortures you will find among these pages. That foul thing is eternal in a way we cannot even begin to comprehend. It cannot be killed in the way that we think of life and death, but we can keep it from entering this realm. We can keep its young, even its influence, from this world. I am one of the keepers of that threshold through which it must step in order to make itself flesh. Hank, you are the last piece of the key. The key it has been building for centuries. The key to open the door and walk into this world. And if that happens then not even God can save us," a darkness overtook Phyllis as she spoke; a shadow which seemed to come from nowhere. She spoke with deadly purpose and both of the Ramseys knew that she was not playing around.

They sat there absorbing what Phyllis had said for a few seconds and then Hank opened his mouth to talk, but before the first syllable passed his lips there was a loud explosion which shook the entire trailer. Hank found himself being flung across the trailer, smashing his entire body against the back wall opposite the front door. Then there was darkness as he lost consciousness.

*W*hen Hank came to he noticed that the trailer was on fire, a rapidly growing conflagration that already threatened to consume them. Phyllis and Amy were already on their feet as he was lying on the floor. The two women helped him stand and Hank saw that the wall which he had been sitting next to was virtually gone. The bits of siding which hung to what remained of the wall were melting. He saw through the hole that Phyllis' propane tank had exploded, leaving the trailer all but destroyed. They were all lucky to be alive.

As they got out into the front yard and away from the smoke and flames Hank spotted a truck some distance down the street. He saw that it was parked and the passenger side door was open and a man was standing behind the door.

There was a loud crack as if the sky itself split in half. Then Hank and Amy found that they were both covered in splattered gore. Phyllis' head had exploded in a red mist. Nearly half of her head and all of her face were completely gone and Hank and Amy were wearing the majority of her brains.

They were in absolute shock. As Hank had opened his mouth to speak pieces of the back to Phyllis's head flew in, coating his tongue in a thick bloody mess. Hank spat chunks of Phyllis out of his mouth and they wasted no time in getting to their car, starting it and driving as fast as they could away from the truck, leaving the twitching, half-headless corpse of the old woman without a second thought. Their fight or flight instincts had kicked in and they knew that it was a flight situation as they had nothing with which to combat a high powered hunting rifle.

When they were sure that the truck was not pursuing them in any way they took the chance on returning to their home. As they pulled into the driveway Hank finally found the ability to speak, which for the preceding few minutes had seemed totally unavailable to him.

"Amy, I'm pretty sure that was Alan's truck. Do you think that he would kill his own aunt? I mean, what the fuck are we in the middle of?" his voice croaked like a pubescent teenager's, he was trembling in fear, still shocked at the sight of Amy and of himself in the mirror. Covered in gore as they were he thought again how lucky they were to have escaped that ordeal with their lives.

"Hank, it might have been Alan's truck, I can't say for sure. But what are the odds that that would happen after you got that phone call? Is Alan involved with Jared's people? Is everyone in this whole town against us?" she had so many questions flowing through her head.

"Amy, I didn't get the book. Did you?" Hank asked her with a slight panic to his voice.

"No Hank, I forgot it. I think Phyllis was holding it when we got you out of the trailer but then..," she trailed off, remembering the horror of the old woman's brutal death.

They went inside and climbed into the shower together without so much as another word, washing off the blood and chunks of brain and skull.

13

THE DAZE AND THE STRUGGLE

*A*fter a week of being so on edge that they couldn't take it anymore, Hank and Amy called Jared. First, they wanted to get more medication as they were running low on Hank's seizure pills as well as the Valium and Vicodin the two had become wholly dependent on. Amy had unlimited refills on her previous prescription for Vicodin, but she was feeling like having something stronger. Hank wanted his own unlimited refills as well and with all they had been through he felt like he deserved it and would have no problem explaining it to Jared. Second, they knew they needed to talk to Jared in order to set things straight with the Cornbread Mafia. He answered their call and seemed to already be expecting that they reach out to him on both of those accounts.

When he arrived at the house Hank and Amy were out on the front porch. As he climbed the stairs the two put their forefingers to their lips in a motion to let him know to be silent. Hank whispered to Jared, "We saw something, with red eyes, out in the barn again. I think it might be what attacked Amy."

"I have a rifle in my trunk. Let's go take a look," Jared seemed confident in a way that Hank was not. Hank attributed it to Jared having grown up in the country and hunting from a young age.

They approached the barn together after getting Jared's gun out of the trunk of his car along with a couple of beers that were in a styrofoam cooler in the back seat. There was a growling noise coming from the barn, that was for sure. A shadow ran toward them for a moment then turned hard to the right and ran out of a hole in one of the rotting old barn planks. Jared raised his rifle and shot. BLAM! There was a loud, high pitched yelp.

Hank was shocked Jared hit anything at all. All Hank had seen was a blur.

"Just as I thought. Goddamn coyote!" Jared said with a cockiness that made Hank a little uncomfortable.

They approached the dead coyote and Hank saw that coyotes were indeed much smaller animals than he had imagined. In his mind, they were as big as wolves and could carry children away in the night. When he considered himself insane and would not face the truths he now held dear as to the nature of his situation he had told himself that Amy had been attacked by a coyote. But the thing before them lying dead at their feet was no thing of terror, no beast in the night with wicked fangs and the voracious appetite of a pack of wolves. No, this was a pathetic little creature, barely thirty pounds. It looked malnourished and mangy. Hank felt bad for the poor thing. He knew that if he didn't overreact then it would still be alive. He might have even found himself feeding it and taking it in as it seemed much more like a dog, or some other family pet than a cold-blooded killing machine.

Hank held his head down in shame as they headed back to

the porch. He lagged far behind Jared who was already telling Amy all about how he killed the coyote with a one in a million shot right through its eye. She had a disgusted look on her face when Hank got back to the porch. Despite that, she smiled at Hank lovingly as he approached. Amy knew that Hank felt bad that Jared had shot the coyote, it was written all over his face.

They didn't go inside as they usually would when Jared would stop by. This visit had an air of urgency to it. It seemed that all three of them just wanted it to be over. Amy broke what had become an uncomfortable silence by just bluntly cutting straight to the chase.

"We don't have the clones. We can't come up with the clones in time for this year's season. Not soon enough to make it worth it. What can we do to make things right? We'd like to know," Amy was calm and collected as she spoke.

"I will pass all of that along, as well as my recommendation that they give y'all another chance. You two ain't from down here and they need to understand that. I know that you guys will keep your word, but I also know you got in over your head. But at the time there were no other options. I do think that I will be able to work all this out. After all, anything happens to you then they don't get paid at all!" he broke into an authentic laughter, full of mirth. It made Hank and Amy both forget just how dire their situation was.

"And I got all sorts of goodies for you, lots of fun stuff," Jared said. He had brought a small backpack up on the porch with him. He unzipped it and gave Hank and Amy both several bottles of pills. There were Oxycontin, Vicodin, Valium, Percaset, muscle relaxers and plenty more of Hank's seizure medicine. He pulled out his prescription pad and wrote them both new prescriptions for everything he had just given them. Hank saw on one of his pill bottles that it said, Dr. Jared Hickman. It only then occurred to Hank that he had never known Jared's last name. He found that extremely odd. But even odder than that was the fact that Jared was a Hickman. Hank tried to hide the surprise on his face. He knew he had a bad poker face, so he sat the pill bottle aside on the porch.

Everything which they had worked up in their minds to be so tense and stressful had suddenly become non-issues. It was such a relief to both of the Ramseys that they were both over-whelmed by a calmness and ease of mind that neither had known in what seemed like years. They had at least some sort of diplomatic channel with the Cornbread Mafia and they had all of their prescription pill needs met. Other than living in a nightmare house full of ghosts and demons things were going great for them.

Jared came by more often than usual over the next few months and had come with good word back from the Corn-bread Mafia. They were willing to let Hank off the hook for that year's season but expected the full ten thousand clones, for the next year, by late February so that they could have large enough plants to put out by late April. Everything which Hank had produced for them up to that point would be taken as the cost of his mistake. He felt that was more than fair and was just relieved to have all of his limbs, fingers, and toes intact.

With such good news and little left in the way of his happi-ness, Hank paid little attention to how many pills he was eating. He began to have severe withdrawal symptoms when he did not have his cocktail of various medications. Amy was much the same, drifting ever deeper into her own addiction. As they both fell into their own abyss they drifted apart emotionally, mentally and spiritually. Amy had returned to the mode of thinking that Hank was a burden and she deserved happiness in her life and that happiness was impossible with the burden of

Hank in her life. Hank spent much of his time so wasted that he wasn't altogether there anymore. Between the toll the seizures were taking on his brain and the seizure medication itself he was in a near vegetative state half of the time. With all the other pills he was taking, even when he was capable of communicating with others, Hank was thoroughly stoned. He lived in a perpetual pilled out illusion. It didn't seem to bother him much but Amy wanted more from life. To Hank being so high all the time was a reprieve from Larvamog, from the ghosts of the house, from the horrible death of Phyllis.

One day when Hank was upstairs tending to his crop of indoor cannabis he heard a familiar voice. At first, he ignored it but it persisted until he had to acknowledge Quan was present. "Hank, you still want to work together? You still want to bring that damn thang down? Well, I'm here," Quan said to ears which did not want to hear him.

It was the first time that Hank had heard one of the ghosts of the house and known who it was, although he still could not see the disembodied voice. Still, he answered, "Yes."

"Hank. That doctor has been having his way with your wife. I done seen it with my own eyes, dead as they are, but they still see better than most. He ain't what he appears to be. Do not trust that man Hank," Quan became a vapor in front of him, semi materializing in a glowing bluish mist. Slowly he became denser in appearance but never stood solidly before Hank, but something close and merely resembling matter.

"I know Quan, I'm not naive. I see what is going on. Really it is none of your business," Hank got defensive with the spirit.

Quan darkened instantly, becoming something more akin to a shadow; a fell spirit of hate. He surged toward Hank, grabbing at his wrists as Hank stepped backward, tripping over one of the hydroponic tables, knocking plants everywhere and spilling gallons of water all over the floor. As Hank was soaking in his hydro solution the ghost was upon him, in his face. It grabbed his right wrist and throat with fingers that burned with an icy chill and in an instant it flew through Hank, right into his chest. He felt his eyes roll back in his head as his chest grew colder than a witches tit in a brass brazier. He gasped for breath but it did not come; like the air had all been vacuumed out of the room. The icy chill spread all through his body. Then Hank became aware that he was not alone in his body anymore.

Hank was now sitting in the back seat of his own experience and Quan was now the one driving. Hank could see the road, but he did not have his hands on the wheel. Quan forced them onto Hank's feet and kicked over the rest of the hydro setup. He knocked over hundreds of plants, worth thousands of dollars, as Hank watched through his own eyes in horror. Every dollar he was going to make for the next four to six months was now dying on the floor of his grow room. Quan laughed through Hank's mouth, a sinister cackle that sounded like he took much pleasure in ruining Hank's life.

The clones for the Cornbread Mafia were in the other room…hopefully, Quan wouldn't go for them. But it was too late. As soon as Hank thought about them then Quan was heading for them. Again Hank watched in horror as several hundred cuttings were mercilessly murdered by Hank's own hand. He began to cry, which was something that Quan could not stop. The tears flowed down Hank's cheeks as he realized that he was set back a couple more months on his ability to provide the clones he owed. This time he might not be treated so well.

With everything gone, all his plants, all his clones, even the freshly cut ones that were just getting rooted, Hank was ruined.

He saw no way out of the hole that he was now in and he began to panic.

He did not know when it was that Quan had left him, he just knew that he awoke on the floor of his grow room. As he looked around he was severely saddened, although not shocked, to see the mess all about him. He fearfully crept down the stairs wondering how it was that Amy and Jared had not heard him upstairs or the commotion that had occurred. He got to the bottom of the stairs and walked down the hall to the kitchen. What Hank saw as he peered through the kitchen doorway shocked him so much that he gasped.

Amy was on her knees on the other side of the kitchen, pleasing Jared with her mouth. As he moaned with ecstatic joy Jared met eyes with Hank just as Amy heard the gasp come in Hank's surprised voice. She knew right then and there she was busted and in that moment she didn't care. Hank staggered back, fell to the ground seizing hard at the same moment that Jared had his pleasure. Amy made sure that Jared was done with his orgasm before turning her attention to Hank.

When they got over to the other side of the kitchen, it became obvious that Hank was going through something unlike any seizure he had experienced before. He shook horribly, his arms stiffened so tightly that Amy thought they would snap their own bones. She rolled Hank over slightly and got his wallet out of his pocket and put it in his mouth so that he didn't bite his tongue off. Hank's eyes were dripping blood at the edges as he spasmed uncontrollably with an unnatural speed which neither Amy nor Jared had ever seen the likes of. Hank went stiff as a board from head to toe and began to float off of the ground. Amy struggled to hold him down but could not. As he reached nearly waist high Jared came over and lent his weight to the struggle, feeling awkward about helping Hank moments after what had just happened.

With Jared's strength, they were finally able to get Hank back down on the floor. He was unconscious so Jared helped Amy put him in their bed. They checked on him every hour or so to make sure he was alright. During the evening Amy recounted much of their supernatural experiences to Jared. Everything she could think of since they had moved in. Everything except for Hank's encounter with Larvamog. She kept that secret to herself as she didn't expect anyone to believe that part of the story. Even someone who had just seen a man floating three feet off of the ground. Ghosts were one thing. Giant, alien, vampire maggots from another dimension were quite another indeed.

14

THE FOX AND THE HOUND

Hank awoke the next morning to a note next to the bed explaining that Amy had gone to work for the day and wouldn't be home until late that evening. As he dragged himself out of bed and into the kitchen for his first cup of coffee of the day there was a loud knock on the front door. Hank didn't care who it was, he just yelled, "Come on in."

He went about making his coffee, lit a cigarette, took a deep breath, sighed and then looked through the house to see who it was that was visiting him so early.

He was happy to see that it was Alan Fox in his living room, sitting on the couch and rolling up a joint. Hank's happiness soon subsided into a look of consternation as he could feel palpable waves of anger coming off of Alan. Something he had never experienced. Alan licked the joint as he finished rolling it, but he did not bring his eyes to bear on Hank. There was a long dramatic pause before he spoke and Hank just stood there in the silence smoking his cigarette. He patted Boris on the head and cleared his throat in a passive-aggressive way, trying to be assertive but failing miserably.

"Hank…you done fucked up. Buoy, you done fucked up bad. Now I heard what happened last night, from Jared. Now I know you wudn't sure who it was you owed all 'em clones to. Well, I'm here to tell ya, it was me 'n my folk. We run shit down here in Marion County. Now we was expectin' oh…ten thousand plants to put out this year and we only got two. That just won't do," Alan was deadly serious as he passed the joint to Hank.

Hank sat down and sighed deeply. He did not speak but inhaled off of the joint deeply, feeling that lifting euphoria that always came with Alan's signature Kentucky outdoor weed. He tried to open his mouth to talk as he passed the joint back to Alan, but he coughed deeply and his face turned beet red. He felt like a newbie; as if he were some high school kid who was trying to impress an old school smoker and making himself look stupid.

"We own you now. Each plant was going to be worth at least two grand to us. That's eight thousand clones times two thousand dollars each. That is sixteen million dollars, Hank. You probly ain't even dreamed of money like 'at have ya? That's a whole crew who don't get paid this season. Let me reiterate buoy…we own you," Alan spoke clearly for him, very calmly and matter-of-factly in a way Hank had never heard him use the English language before.

"What can I do to make this right? Anything…" Hank realized that he was almost crying. His voice creaked with his anxiety.

"Give me every damn dollar you got right now Hank. There's people that's got to eat and pay their bills," Alan didn't hesitate, but he did pass Hank the doobie while he spoke.

Country folk had a way of keeping things cordial and using manners even when making threats of death. It struck Hank as something out of Gone with the Wind, very southern gentle-manly while being an absolute dick.

"I have thirty-eight hundred bucks. I have another twelve hundred and fifty on the street. I know that ain't much, but it's all I have," Hank was nearly sobbing as he wiped tears from the corners of his eyes. He tried to play it off as if he had gotten smoke in his eyes.

'Ok. I'm goin' ta take Boris with me. I'm fighting him tonight down at ol' man Jenkins's farm. Place a bet against Boris with every dollar you got buoy. If you can double 'at measly five grand you got…well it would double yer chances of livin' through the situation," Alan laughed jovially as if they were watching a comedy movie or fishing. As if they were doing something totally mundane and not considering Hank's possible fate.

"Alan, I can't do that. Boris is Amy's dog, he's her baby. Anything but that," Hank begged with little dignity left in his voice.

He turned his back on Alan and walked into the kitchen, knowing it was probably a bad idea. He finally made his cup of coffee, his hand trembling as he struggled to put in the excessive cream and sugar that he was used to. With his coffee, he took his first round of pills for the day. Painkillers, Valium, muscle relaxers, seizure meds. He took a handful of various colored little tablets. As he choked them down he heard Alan approaching, his footsteps reverberating through the house. The boots on hardwood floor sound made Hank think of the old spaghetti westerns his dad used to watch. When he turned to face Alan he saw that there was a pistol pointed at him.

"Nothin' personal Hank, but I don't give two fucks whose

dog it is. I'm takin' him. This is non-negotiable. I will bring what little is left of him back to you tonight before Amy gets home from work. You will say coyotes got him. Got it?" Alan was stone cold.

Hank could only nod in agreement as he began to panic. Alan left, half of the joint he rolled still smoking away in the ashtray. He took Boris with him as he left. It was obvious that he had brought a dog leash with him just to lead the dog out. As Hank watched from the porch Alan loaded Boris up into his truck and soon they were gone. Hank fell to his knees crying. He knew what it would do to Amy. He knew what it was doing to his own self. Losing Boris was losing one-third of the little family that they had built. He was the only pet they had left since Hank let his aquariums fall into chaos. When all of his fish died he swore off aquariums, which although designed and intended to relieve stress only compounded it. Boris was differ-ent. He had become much more than a family pet to Amy and he was one of the best dogs Hank had ever had as far as temperament and behavior. In that moment Hank felt more helpless than he ever had before in his life.

He called everyone that owed him money and was able to come up with four hundred more dollars. He had never been to a dogfight before and he didn't want to go, but if it was going to save his life and/or the life of Amy then he would do it. Forty-two hundred dollars, that was all he had to give those people. He wondered who else that he knew personally was involved with Alan and his mafia. "I should have known what they were going to do with ten thousand clones. Of course, it was a crop worth tens of millions. What did I get us in the middle of? No, it was Amy that made this deal with them when I was in the hospital. Goddamn it!"

Around sunset, he got a call from Alan to meet at old man

Jenkins's house. It was only a mile away from Hank's own house and he knew right where it was. He didn't have a car and Alan hung up the phone before he could ask for a ride and Hank was stuck walking. By the time he got there he saw that there were about thirty vehicles parked in the yard, which was essentially a field, just like his own yard. Hank walked past all of the cars and found his way to a barn which was full of noise and had floodlights illuminating it inside that were being run from a gas generator. As he walked into the barn he saw that most people were gathered around a makeshift fighting pit and two dogs were tearing each other to pieces in a bloody mess. A man in a filthy trucker's hat and overalls, with only one shoulder buckled, covering his massive belly cleared his throat loud enough for Hank to hear it over the dogfight. He was obviously the doorman.

"We've been expecting you, Hank. Place your bets over there," he said in a voice stale and gravely as he motioned over to a corner where a man was sitting at a table with a bottle of whiskey in front of him. He looked like a farm hand and Hank could not say that he knew the man, which was odd since it was such a small community.

As he approached the table the bet taker poured a shot into a glass and lifted it up, offering it to Hank. Hank took it reluctantly and gulped it down fast, hoping that it didn't have a negative reaction with any of his medications. "Sit," The man said.

"I need to place a bet," was all Hank could think of to say.

"Is that so?" the man chided him. "How much you got and what dog do you want to bet on?"

"I got forty-two hundred. I want to bet everything I got on the dog that is fighting against Boris," Hank tried not to cry.

"Oh, I see. It's like that is it? Alright then. Forty-two

hundred on Zeus. And wouldn't you know it, that is the next fight," the man motioned to the ring where a dead dog was being cleaned up. Hank saw Boris, being held closely by Alan, enter the ring which was still covered in blood and gore.

Then Hank saw Zeus and he shed a tear, which thankfully nobody noticed. Pitch black and thick as a semi truck, Zeus was an obvious veteran fighter. He approached the ring like an old friend. He had soulless eyes and scars all over him. This was a true killing machine. This was why people feared pit bulls. He looked at Boris, who trembled with fear and tried to cower behind Alan's legs. Zeus sat calmly on his back feet, waiting patiently. His owner so confident in the dog's absolute loyalty that he didn't even enter the ring with the black beast of a dog.

Alan took the leash off of Boris and stepped over the barrier out of the ring. A bell dinged and Boris whimpered as Zeus stood up casually and slowly. Hank averted his eyes, he could not watch but the noises he heard told him all he needed to know. Boris did not even put up a fight. Zeus had toyed with him, not even seeing him as a challenge. After the commotion of the crowd subsided and everything was calm again Hank opened his eyes and saw his dog lying in a pool of blood. His fur matted so thick with his own blood that Hank could not believe that he was still breathing, but he was. Alan was having a friend scrape Boris up off of the ground and they put him on a stretcher. Hank followed, in a daze, and watched as they put his dog into the back of Alan's truck.

Alan looked back at Hank and said, "Well come on buoy. We gotta get my dog to the vet. You should call Amy 'n let her know that Boris was attacked by coyotes and that she should meet us in Danville at the veterinary hospital. You're good buddy Alan's got yer back and done gave you a ride."

Hank was flabbergasted. He didn't know what to say. He

just got into the truck's passenger seat and left with Alan. Only when they were down the road did Alan bother to tell him that he didn't need to worry about the prize money from his bet against Boris. It was all taken care of. Hank felt nauseous. He hated Alan more deeply than anyone he had ever known. In that moment he knew for sure that the sadistic madman driving them to the vet was the one driving the truck that had gunned down Phyllis. Hank knew he was in the clutches of a true psychopath and there was nothing he could do about it.

After driving for what seemed like an eternity to Hank they finally came to Danville and the vet's office. Amy was already in the parking lot. Hank forgot that he had called her on the way. She closed the store early and headed to Danville as soon as she got the news about poor Boris.

Everything seemed to occur so fast that Hank didn't seem to notice what was happening, still somewhat in a daze from the traumatic events of the day. Amy and Alan rushed Boris inside, but it was likely that he was already dead. Hank didn't even know that dogs had that much blood in them, let alone that they could lose so much. He stood in the parking lot, next to Alan's truck, smoking a cigarette with shaky hands cold from the summer night's air that was thick with moisture. When his cigarette was done he lit another one off of the butt, smoked half of it and then proceeded inside.

Alan and Amy were just emerging from the back room. Hank could tell by the looks on both of their faces that Boris didn't make it. Amy was crying a steady stream of tears and sobbing uncontrollably. They left the vet's office in silence. Hank went to give Amy a hug in the parking lot but she brushed him away and gave him a look that turned his heart to stone. He knew that she knew the truth. Either Alan had admitted it to her, the vet had figured it out or both. Either way,

Hank knew his marriage was over; Amy conveyed everything she was thinking with one look. A look of absolute disgust as she went to her car. Neither of them said a word to Alan and Amy just nodded her head, indicating to Hank that he was to get into the car with her. He almost failed to notice, he was still in somewhat of a daze.

They rode home in silence. Hank fidgeted with his cigarette lighter nervously. When they got to his house Alan dropped him off without saying a word. As Hank opened the front door he broke down crying, sobbing loudly, choking on his words. He began to hyperventilate as he gasped, failing to form words. Not that they would have done any good.

He went straight for the living room, intending to sleep on the couch. He was surprised when Amy spoke, "We are done, Hank. I don't know if it is for good. I don't know if we will ever repair this marriage, but as of now, we are done. I'm going to call mom tomorrow and see about going to Illinois for a while to live with her. Or maybe I'm going to go back to Lexington. I haven't decided yet, but I am getting the fuck out of here Hank and for right now I don't want to be with you anymore. I'm going to give it some time, but I might be filing for divorce." As Amy's words found Hank's ears he knew that she had practiced every word of the speech on the way home from the veterinarian's office. It was too well organized of a speech for such a heavily emotional thing to say. Hank understood that it was way more than just Boris, but that losing Boris was also more than she could bear to take. It would crack her like an egg no matter what kind of foundation their marriage rested upon.

He nodded in agreement, got a blanket and pillow out of the closet in the den and sacked out on the living room couch as Amy retired to the bedroom. It wasn't long before he realized that Amy must have had those words, or something very similar, prepared for a long time. Boris's tragic death was just the straw that broke the camel's back. Or rather the cement truck that broke the camel's back.

Hank knew that he was much weaker without Boris and Amy. Without his family. He knew that he was wide open for attack from every form his mental illness was taking. Ghosts, demons, redneck hillbillies. Every threat to his health and sanity seemed to mesh into one paranoia in his mind. He was as afraid of the things in the woods as he was of the Cornbread Mafia and he knew that made him insane. Again he gave up on everything he was holding onto, embracing mental illness as the only sane explanation. With Amy leaving he would be alone. Alone in the house to face his nightmares and fears, to endure his seizures and to grow the clones for people who would kill him if he didn't.

As he huddled on the couch Hank felt more alone than he ever had in his life. He realized that he should have seen the situation with Boris was a setup. "What do these people want from me? If it was really all about business then they woulda just killed me."

Hankwas alone with all of his thoughts and even before he fell asleep he descended into a nightmare. He smelled the foul, acrid stench of his basement seeping up through the floor. It carried on its back a tinge of that strange and sickening musk of the giant maggot-demon Larvamog. Hank told himself that he was just freaked out after the day's events but the smell drove him mad as the hours passed on.

He finally fell asleep not long before dawn. He dreamed only of drowning in a sea of black sludge, unable to breathe or swim through it; he suffocated until he awoke. Amy was already in the kitchen making coffee and was on her phone, already making arrangements to get help moving.

15

THE APPRENTICE, THE JUNKIE AND
THE MICROBIOLOGIST

*A*fter Amy left him, Hank fell into a depression that he found difficult to comprehend. He had never felt so low, especially since Amy saw Boris's blood on Hank's hands. Being in such a low place, constantly feeling the weight of his financial ruin and having nobody to turn to Hank became extremely susceptible to being overtaken by Quan. There were days when he would experience most of his waking time completely under the control of the mad spirit of the railway-man. It was not easy for him to admit to himself that it was happening and he chalked it all up to his own madness. Insanity again being the only rational explanation for what he experienced.

During those dark times when he was not wholly in control, he was aware of what his body was doing. Quan had more or less decided to leave his life alone. No more explosive outbursts like the one that ruined Hank's crop. Not only had Quan ruined Hank's financial future, but his marriage had fallen apart as a result and he was still beholden to the Cornbread

Mafia. Hank had to constantly remind himself that Quan might be a personality that his own brain had devised after dealing with trauma, but he was completely capable of bringing absolute ruin to his life. He no longer even considered the possibility that he was dealing with real events, that he lived in a house of ghosts and demons, that he lived where the most heinous things had occurred and left their imprint upon the fabric of reality.

The life that Hank had imagined had slipped right through his fingers and he found himself in a pit of despair. Nothing seemed to matter to him, even his grow room and his clones were little solace from the overwhelming mountain of fear and paranoia that consumed his life when he wasn't possessed by the builder of the house.

He began trading his highest grade marijuana for heroin. Hank's desperation found some ease with stronger drugs. Still, he consumed a substantial amount of pills, but heroin became his favorite thing quickly. He could drift away into another land, where there was no pain and no paranoia. The locals he had been selling weed to since he moved to Gravel Switch were more than happy to trade with him and there seemed to be no shortage. No shortage and steady trade partners meant little chance of a dry spell and therefore withdrawals. He knew that even if it did come to all that then he could stave off any symptoms of dope sickness with his prescription opiates.

Living on the edge of death and sanity Hank no longer cared about things such as his seizures getting in the way of driving. He could care less if he wrecked and so he bought himself a Jeep Cherokee to get around. Without Amy to drive him places what choice did he have? He had always liked driving and even after he started having regular seizures he would take country drives with Amy. They had a system worked out where if he felt a seizure coming on he would slow down, pull over and she would take the wheel from him as he applied the brake. They had practiced it so many times it had become rote. He had to remind himself that he could no longer rely on her. He often thought of just driving head-on into a semi truck, but never quite found the compulsion to overcome his cowardice.

After a few months of living alone he had gotten his grow room up and running again, despite all the hell Quan had wrecked upon it. Hank found the duties of producing the clones for Alan and the Cornbread Mafia to be about as much as he could handle by himself. He also had to produce a crop of finished flowers to continue paying his rent and bills and to eventually come out of debt. While visiting his friends in Lexington, the Wilsons, he was introduced by Chris to a young man of nineteen named Lief Gutsell. Chris had explained to Hank on the phone before he went to town that Lief might make a good helper or apprentice for Hank. Chris had figured out all of the details before Hank even got to his house after the two-hour drive to what seemed like Hank to be the "Big City" after so much time in Gravel Switch.

Lief would live with Hank, as a rent-paying roommate. He would look after Hank as a caretaker and be there in case medical assistance was needed. In exchange, he would help Hank grow his crop and Lief would be taught everything about growing cannabis and also be taught how to blow glass if Hank was up to it. All of it sounded too good to be true to Hank. The kid was even willing to let Hank have all of his glass work that he produced for the first year of his apprenticeship under him. With all of the details ironed out, Hank realized that all that remained to be seen was whether or not he was compatible with Lief.

Hank was happy to find that they were compatible indeed. They sat up for hours at Chris Wilson's house, even after Chris had gone to bed himself, talking about B-grade horror films from the nineteen seventies and eighties. Lief even loved Hank's favorite psychedelic jam bands and also knew a lot about old school punk rock groups that Hank had listened to in his younger years but had always been afraid to share with Amy. Hank had found a kindred spirit in Lief and it made him feel just alive enough that he realized that he wanted to grow, he wanted to progress, he wanted to live and to love and to be happy. Most of all he wanted to get the debt paid to the Cornbread Mafia and Lief was the perfect instrument to help him achieve that goal.

They wasted no time getting started and got Lief moved down to Gravel Switch and situated within a week. To show his gratitude to his loyal old friend Hank gave Chris two ounces of his top-shelf marijuana. The stuff he always reserved for his own head stash. Chris was extremely thankful and explained that it would save him a lot of money over the next couple of months. It really was no big deal to Hank and he was glad to do it. In that moment he remembered why it was that he did what he did. He had always loved that sense of family that came from the hippie scene. He remembered a time long before then when he had given someone else the shoes off of his own feet because that person had cuts and bruises all over their own naked feet and still had many miles to walk. Hank, for the first time in years, felt once again truly in touch with his own values. He considered that perhaps Amy leaving him might have been the best thing to happen to him.

Lief had immediately noticed that Hank was unable to get rid of Amy's presence in the house, even if he had wanted to which he clearly did not. Amy had become a terrible hoarder and took little to nothing with her when she left the house. Hank had assumed that she meant to come back to him some-day. But with Lief there he seemed to just want the space to himself so that he could move forward with his endeavors. The new kid was great at helping him to pack her stuff up. All the random things that she had hoarded over the years that they had lived out there were put in boxes and Rubbermaid tubs and put away out in the two shacks in the backyard. Hank found quite a bit of piece of mind when his space felt like his own again and not a reminder of some past conflict. He had felt like he had been living in a Holocaust memorial or a shrine to some war long ago.

Lief, to Hank's surprise, did not judge Hank at all for his heroin use. He understood it to be just another opiate, the strongest opiate Hank could get. As far as Lief was concerned Hank was suffering terribly from a horrible disease and needed all the help he could get to deal with it. The relief Hank felt at the situation made him all the more comfortable with the new kid.

Lief was lanky and tall, a good six inches taller than Hank was. He had dark hair, a shade of brown that was almost black that he kept in a tight ponytail which almost reached his waist. His face was slightly long, like a horse's face a bit and he talked a little too fast for Hank's liking but it wasn't a problem. Everything Hank showed him about growing cannabis he absorbed like a sponge taking in water. The young man was a natural. When they went out to the garage and Hank fired up his glass blowing torch and turned on his kiln for the first time in months he saw that blowing glass suited Lief just as well as growing marijuana. The Gutsell family had quite a large fortune and were well known in Lexington and the surrounding areas. They bred thoroughbred Arabian horses as the family business but Lief had wanted nothing to do with it. Still, they were happy to give him all that he needed financially and emotionally in order to pursue his goals of becoming a glass blower and a cannabis grower. His father had been at Woodstock when he was a kid and his mother had lived in the Haight Ashbury in the early seventies, although she hardly remembered it. They were very non-judgmental and Lief was thankful for their support. He had other friends with parents which were much older, like his own. But they were usually not so open-minded; nor were they usually as liberal.

Because of their own hippie background, Lief's parents loved Hank and were tickled to death that he was willing to take their son on as an apprentice. Their own Bohemian world-view and child-rearing environment had lead to the perfect storm for Hank. Everything was getting done. Alan was getting paid, Hank didn't even have to look at him. He just gave Lief tray after tray of cuttings when they were rooted and the apprentice drove them over to Alan's house. Hank was nearly caught up on his quota by the February due date, though he still was short two thousand clones. Alan informed Lief that it wouldn't be a problem and that Hank had stepped things up in a way that the Cornbread Mafia neither foresaw nor expected. They conveyed to Lief that they were going to adopt a much more lenient stance with Hank.

After Hank had been working with the young man for a few months Lief had more than tripled his revenue stream. The apprentice had quite a few customers in the Lexington area and they loved the quality of Hank's product. More than just smokers and casual users, Lief opened up channels to distributors. It wouldn't be long until Hank was looking at having all debts paid to the Cornbread Mafia, at least the ones that they had overtly revealed. He would never forget that Alan Fox had told him that he was owned by them. He knew there was more to his debt than simply just the cuttings he had to root. Still, he wondered what terrible price they might ask him to pay, "Was Boris not enough?"

After a very long day of working in the grow room and dipping cuttings into the rooting solution, planting them in rockwool growing medium and placing them in humidity trays Hank and Lief decided to take the night off and go into town and hit some strip clubs.

Rather than go to Danville to the one bar that was topless they drove on, to Lexington, and had their pick of several establishments. Hank had never been to a strip club, but he wasn't going to tell that to his apprentice. Even though it was a twenty-one and over club Lief found it easy to get in just based on the fact that he was a Gutsell and his father knew the owner. At least that is what he told the doorman, but whether or not it was true Lief neither knew nor cared. The club was called Pure Gold: A Gentleman's Club. Upon entering the place Hank was sure that there were no actual gentlemen in the vicinity. Just greasy older men in sweatpants who stared lustfully, drooling over topless women less than half their ages. They took seats at the main stage as a gorgeous young black woman in leather bondage gear did a pole dance that gave Lief an erection and would have given Hank one if he were still capable without medication. Still, he had brought a Viagra just in case he was lucky enough to take home a stripper.

A well endowed topless waitress approached them and took their drink orders. Hank had a beer and Lief got a whiskey and coke. They both found it hard to make eye contact with her as they drooled over her large yet supple breasts. When she brought their drinks Hank tipped her fifty percent of the tab and got forty dollars in dollar bills for two twenties. He felt dumb for not bringing small bills to a strip club.

They took turns putting a few singles into the bondage belt that the dancer was wearing. She gave them a show and seated herself right in front of them and spread her legs far apart, sliding slightly off the stage toward them as she did. They could smell her feminine juices from that distance. When they stopped showering her with one dollar bills she turned her attention elsewhere before she was called off stage and the next dancer came out from behind a black velvet curtain.

This time she was a white girl, short with green eyes and olive skin. Hank could see that she was a blonde, even though she dyed her hair an electric blue-green her eyebrows were very light. As she danced she would often look over and make eye contact with Hank. Halfway through her performance, by the time she was nearly naked, Hank realized that he knew her from high school. Her name was Amanda Wexler and he had once had an extreme crush on her in the ninth grade. She was a year older than he was and was a sophomore when he was a freshman. He couldn't count the times that he had fantasized about her. He was glad to see that time had been kind to her body and she still had firm c-cup breasts and a round butt. As all that occurred to him, he found himself staring into her eyes as she danced, even though he could have beheld any part of her that he wished.

As she was finishing she turned his direction and mouthed the words, "I know you!" excitedly at him. As the next dancer took the stage she came out into the front of the house, got a drink at the bar and came right up to Hank, unabashedly still topless although she wore a thong and stiletto boots. "Hanky Ramsey, you look great!" she threw herself around his neck, hugging him in such a way that her bare breasts were right in his face as he sat there helplessly smothered. She laughed and then backed up from the waist and leaned in and gave him a kiss on the cheek. "Damn, you smell good too!" she said as she laughed about the fact that he smelled like weed and everyone in the place probably knew he was holding.

"Amanda, so good to see you! Meet my friend Lief, Lief Gutsell," Hank felt awkward speaking to Amanda under such circumstances. Still, he was sure happy to have a gorgeous woman showing him affection. He had even felt somewhat of a stir in his pants as she had rubbed her breasts on his face. He had always wondered what her nipples had been like and he was not disappointed. His cheek still tingled from their soft caress.

"Nice to meet you, sweetheart," she extended her hand to Lief who took it loosely and shook it very gently. She leaned in and gave him a kiss on the cheek as well. As she did so leaning across Hank, her left nipple brushing slightly against his face again. This time teasing his lips. As she lingered just a moment too long to kiss Lief Hank thought about just opening his mouth ever so slightly. He needed to taste her tit. He needed to taste all of her. He became aware that he had a rock solid erection in his pants.

"I need to go get dressed. I'm off now if you wanna catch up Hanky," she said as she pouted her lips at him slightly. He could feel himself getting warm, his pulse quickening.

"I would love to sweetheart. We'll be right here. You just take your time and when you are done we can go burn one if you want to. You still smoke weed don't you?" he felt unusually calm for such a situation. It had been fifteen years since he had been with anyone but Amy and he thought that nervousness was appropriate. Instead, he felt confident and it was obvious that she was picking up on it. He was sure that he could take her home.

Hank ordered another beer as he waited on Amanda to return from the dressing room. He watched the next two acts before she was back. Lief got a lap dance from a Mexican girl who looked like she might have been too young to have worked in such a place, at such a profession. Hank had to remind himself that Lief was only nineteen himself and that it wasn't weird at all.

When Amanda returned she was dressed normally, as Hank remembered. She was wearing blue jeans with ripped up knees and a Primus t-shirt. No longer wearing the stilettos she had on a pair of Nike running shoes. Even though her outward appearance had done a one hundred and eighty-degree turn she came back as flirtatious as ever. She made Hank stand up so that she could give him a full body hug. When she felt the press of his erection against her own crotch she pressed him in closer to her, grinding on him hard. He squeezed her with both hands and she bit his earlobe a bit. Teasing him.

"Last I heard, you were married, Hank. What brings you into a place like this?" she asked but he could tell that she really didn't care either way what the answer was.

"I'm not divorced...yet. Amy and I split up a while back. This is actually the first night that I have gone out since the breakup," he didn't feel like holding anything back. For some reason Amanda made him feel really comfortable.

They hung out in the club for another hour. Talking the entire time Amanda and Hank ignored Lief for the most part. The didn't even seem to notice when he went in the back to the VIP area with the girl who had been giving him lap dances. They did seem to take notice though when he returned, looking exhausted and sweating profusely.

When Lief got back to the table Hank informed him that Amanda would be coming back to Gravel Switch with them for the weekend. Lief had no problem with that and the three of them left the club together. The apprentice drove the Jeep and Hank and Amanda talked the entire time. Even though they had never been really close and Hank always had assumed that she looked at him like a social pariah in high school they still found plenty to talk about on the ride back to Gravel Switch. Lief found it hard to believe that they weren't extremely close old friends.

Amanda had never married, never had kids. She had graduated from UK with a master's in microbiology but found it a difficult field. Not because there was no work or because she couldn't get hired, but because she was sick of seeing men who were less educated and less productive than her making more money to do the same job, simply because they were men. That is why she loved stripping. She found it empowering, fun and erotic. She could work less, make more and exploit the same men who she used to be treated as unequal to. It was the perfect job for her, but she knew that sooner or later it wouldn't pay the bills anymore. Nobody wanted to look at a geriatric stripper, so Amanda had been squirreling away money for her retirement. She invested in stocks and had a pretty good savings in her account. She might have been a stripper, but Amanda Wexler was not stupid. She would take care of herself, even if the world would not.

When they got back to the house Lief was opening the front door when he noticed that Hank and Amanda were already making out. Lief figured that they would go immediately to Hank's room, but to his surprise, they followed him into the living room. Amanda was quite impressed with Hank's place. He could tell by the way she took in the high doors and vaulted ceilings, how she oohed and ahhed at the sight of the vintage fixtures and the chandelier in the foyer. But more so than with the house she was impressed with Hank's cannabis.

As he rolled up a couple of joints for them to smoke he packed her a bowl just for herself. "So you can catch up to us," Hank said. She smiled from ear to ear after hitting the pipe. Lief just sat there, quietly, smiling as well as he remembered the fun he had just had with the stripper Cinnamon. It had only cost him seventy-five bucks. That was his favorite part.

As they got good and stoned Lief decided to give the two of them some room and he retired for the evening. As soon as he left Amanda and Hank started making out again, sprawling on the couch. He had dreamed of the moment since high school and was still a little confused as to why a woman as hot as Amanda would have any interest in him. He decided to just go with it and keep up the air of confidence he was feeling, despite how unnatural it seemed.

They took their time with foreplay, as they both seemed to be in no hurry and were enjoying themselves. When Hank felt that she was sufficiently teased he unbuttoned her pants and laid her back onto the couch. He pulled off each of her shoes, taking a moment to massage her feet in turn. He slid her pants off and stood back for a moment, soaking in the beauty of her body, the curve of her legs and hips. He spread her legs apart and buried his face right in her crotch, pushing her thong aside with his tongue. He licked her and sucked her until she came more times than he had ever made a woman come; at least in his mind. She didn't let out much noise, which he was thankful for as he didn't want to wake his young roommate. Still, he was sure that she was satisfied and he pulled off his own pants and climbed on top of her. She reached down to grab his penis and was surprised that it was both limp, even after the hot action he had just given her, and quite small. Hank could tell by her reaction that she was a bit disappointed by his size. Still, he prided himself on his cunnilingus skills, he knew she was satisfied. If she couldn't get off on his manhood then he wouldn't feel bad for her. He had gotten used to the feeling of rejection he had gotten from girls in high school when they noticed how small he really was, but it had been many years since then and Amy had always seemed to enjoy him despite his size. He wondered if she had just been lying to him. He wondered if he had been lying to himself.

Hank realized that he had drifted off into a daze, half from the opiates he was on and half just from his wandering thoughts. He looked down and saw that Amanda had him in her mouth, trying in vain to make his soldier salute. After a solid five minutes of sucking, stroking and tonguing his flaccid cock she gave up.

He spent the next half hour explaining how he had gotten to such a place physically. How his seizure medication would mess with his ability to perform sexually, sometimes leaving him completely impotent. He could see that she was not really that upset by the situation and had more pity for him than anger, but he kept talking and talking, making excuse after excuse. As he talking in circles she chimed in, interrupting the flow of his thoughts. "We can get you some Viagra or something. It might help. I'd love to try again sweetie."

He remembered then that he had a Viagra in his pocket. He didn't even speak to her, he jumped up, grabbed his pants and pulled the pill out. When he had it in hand he brandished it like a magician finishing a trick and gave a whispered (so as not to wake Lief), "Ta-da!"

She smiled at him with excitement. He popped the pill and went to the kitchen to get some water. As he was drinking he felt his hands tremble. Hank felt the icy chill of the grave set over him and his eyes rolled back in his head. He was afraid that he was about to have a seizure but soon realized that Quan had once again taken up residence in his body. Hank looked down at his hands in horror, realizing that Quan was now in control and he had a beautiful woman ready to make love to him in the other room.

Amanda had taken a vibrating dildo out of her purse while Hank was in the kitchen and began masturbating with it, trying to keep herself turned on while Hank's Viagra was kicking in. She was shocked to see that when he came back into the room he was a completely changed man. He stared at her as a predator stares down its prey. She felt immediately turned on and motioned for him to come to her as she spread her legs far apart, showing him the vibrator sliding in and out of her as she groaned slightly, playfully for him.

He wasted no time and when he got to her he was as stiff as a board. He plunged right into her and she purred. She spent the next hour and a half being ravaged by him in ways that she never thought possible. Amanda lost count of her orgasms after they hit double digits. Hank didn't say a word to her, he just grunted animalistically and smacked her backside. He took her in every position that she could even fathom existed.

When he finally finished she was almost relieved, she felt absolutely worn out. He sat there on the couch next to her for a moment, rubbing her legs. He lit a cigarette, took a few drags and handed it to her. As she finished the smoke he rolled another joint up. Once he lit it he turned to look at Amanda and spoke in a voice that she was unsure of. It seemed to be a bit deeper than his voice and she thought that he was joking around.

"So, when're ya movin' in, doll?" Quan spoke the words

with Hank's mouth, but Hank didn't care. He wanted Amanda to stay around more than anything he could imagine. She was comforting for him in every possible way. Hank didn't mind Quan being in charge when it came to sex if he was going to perform like that! It really didn't matter who was in control of the body, the brain still felt the pleasure either way.

"How about right now then?" Amanda answered without hesitation. "I see that you have a boner again Hanky. Why don't you come here and see if I can't help you with that." And then Hank got the best blowjob he had ever had in his entire life.

Everything was coming together sweet for him. The only obstacle would be to see if she would deal with his heroin use, but hell, for her he would quit the drug in a heartbeat. He decided to sleep on whether or not to tell her about his addiction or to simply kick heroin and supplement his use with the Vicodin and Oxycontin that he had in abundance.

They fell asleep naked on the couch in each other's arms, much to the annoyance of Lief who in the morning couldn't help but wonder what fluids had gotten all over the couch. He woke them up by brewing a pot of coffee and letting the smell waft through the house.

16

THE WRITER AND THE THIEF

*A*manda awoke naked the next morning to the smell of coffee. She was still in Hank's arms and found that to be comfortable. She hoped that he was joking about moving in with him, although she did love the house and the land. It would be too far from her work at Pure Gold to make the commute, but it wasn't out of the question to date Hank. After all, he had pleasured her in ways that she was sure she had never been pleasured before. It was shocking to her when she looked back on it as she sat up and wiped the sleep out of her eyes. Hank started to stir as she got her clothes on.

When they were both awake and had lit up the first cigarette of the day and poured their coffee they heard the sound of the shower turning on in the bathroom and were immediately reminded that Lief was there. Hank was all smiles and beamed from ear to ear. With his coffee, he took all of his medications for the morning and doubled up on his painkillers so that he could begin to wean himself off of heroin. They had a perfectly normal morning and enjoyed a breakfast of bacon and scrambled eggs. They made extra for Lief who was happy that he didn't have to cook for himself. Hank made it clear that he would give Amanda a ride back to Lexington any time that she needed but that she was welcome to hang out for the day, or even the weekend. She was a little disappointed to find out that he had a lot to do in his grow room and in the glass shop in the garage, though she thought that it might be interesting to just have time to relax out in the country and it would only be for the day. They could have the night to themselves again, which excited Amanda quite a bit.

It was noon before Hank and Lief came down from upstairs. They had spent all morning trying to get the pH and the parts per million of total dissolved solids both just right in his hydroponic solution tank. If the pH was off all of his plants would essentially not take up nutrients properly and if there was too much nutrient in the water then they would over fertilize the plants. Hank explained it all to Amanda during lunch as they smoked a joint before he took Lief out to the glass shop. Amanda listened intently and then embarrassed Hank a little when after five minutes of Hank rambling about his grow operation she reminded him that she was a microbiologist and basic hydroponics was elementary to her. He had been excited to share his knowledge base but the tables had turned on him and he felt a bit silly to have assumed that she was uneducated because she was a stripper. He could tell that he lost a few points with her over that, but wasn't too concerned as he figured that she got that a lot.

Amanda had spent the morning walking around the farm. She checked out the barn and the creek, the slave quarters and the garage. Otherwise, there were only the fields and the surrounding hills. She got bored a little quicker than she thought she would and went back to the house to see what she could find to do.

She was shocked to see how few books Hank actually owned. Amanda was an avid reader and Hank obviously was not. He had some of C.S. Lewis' Narnia books and The Lord of the Rings trilogy but otherwise, most of his books were about growing cannabis or the Haight Ashbury in the nineteen sixties. She looked through the living room bookshelf and eventually on the bottom shelf, under all the other books she found a horror novel to read. She had never heard of it but Amanda was looking forward to devouring How Dear the Dawn by Marc Elliot.

Amanda found it to be a surprisingly good read, nothing like the other vampire novels that she had read. No flowery romances or Victorian settings, just pure terror. Reading it allowed her to spend the better part of the morning entertained. Hank came downstairs around eleven and asked her to go to Kentucky Fried Chicken in Perryville and get lunch. She was more than happy to do it as she didn't really know the area and wanted to get out and stretch her legs. Driving had always helped Amanda think and she had a lot to process. What were the odds that a boy she had a crush on in high school would just fall into her lap like Hank did? She chalked it up to kismet.

After lunch, Amanda got extremely bored. One novel a day was enough. She decided to go upstairs to see Hank's plants since he was outside in the garage blowing glass. The thought crossed her mind of having him make her a dildo. Handblown glass dildos were extremely expensive and were all the rage among her friends. Hell, she knew she could help Hank sell a ton of them.

As she got to the top of the steps that wound up to the second floor like a tightly coiled snake, she noticed that she was in a large room and the grow room was off to the left. But it was the room that was off to the right that called her. Amanda didn't know why but she just felt compelled to go into the room. Her spine tingled a bit and she wondered if it were a place she was not supposed to go.

When she opened the door Amanda saw a menagerie of odds and ends from various time periods. There was a desk with an old typewriter on it. An old wheelchair that looked like it had come straight from a sanitarium sat in the corner. Tie-dyed tapestries hung on the walls, seeming very out of place. There were trunks and chests which were obvious relics from the nineteenth century as well as an old standing mirror covered with a cloth. Of everything in the room though she was most affected by the doll which sat in the wheelchair. It was a wretched thing, rotting and nasty. It exuded a foulness that she could not explain and Amanda took one of the tie-dyes down from the wall and put it over the doll so that she didn't have to look at it.

After the doll was covered Amanda felt comfortable again. She laughed at herself because she wasn't a superstitious person. She didn't believe in ghosts or spirits and she damn sure wasn't scared of some old creepy doll. Even as she told herself that she knew she was lying to herself. It had evoked such a strong reaction in her, she just knew that she didn't want to be near it, didn't want to even look at it.

Amanda knelt down by the desk upon which the typewriter sat. She opened a drawer to find a ream of yellowed old paper. "How fortunate!", she thought. Writing was a passion of her's and she thought it would be fun to type a poem or a short story on the antique typewriter. As she wound a piece of paper through the feed she realized that it probably wouldn't work, that the ink was probably dry if the arms and keys weren't too rusty to operate.

To Amanda's surprise, it worked just fine. She was elated at the sound of the keys hammering onto the page. A sound she had grown up with but as she became an adult the computer took the place of the typewriter. She marveled at how her favorite writers had all used the typewriter, doing manually what she struggled to do digitally. She felt spoiled, thinking of Stephen King writing a seventeen hundred page book on a manual typewriter, hunting and pecking as she had heard he did.

She soon began to write an erotic short story about what she had experienced the night before with Hank. She made it as nasty and visceral as she possibly could and had a fun time doing it. Hank had certainly inspired her. After writing for an hour or so she realized that she had been in quite a deep trance for quite some time. That was the zone that she wanted to be in. That was where the magic really happened when it came to writing. When Amanda got in her zone she could write all day and hardly even notice. She had often thought of giving up stripping for novel writing just as she had given up microbiology for stripping. Something about the old typewriter just really seemed to resonate with her. Amanda felt much more comfortable on the old contraption than she did on her own computer.

As she typed she became aware of a presence behind her. She had assumed that it was Hank and chose to playfully ignore him. When he put his hand on her shoulder a chill ran through her whole body. A chill that touched her heart itself and set deep in the bone. Amanda felt faint and woozy. She reached up to take his hand off of her shoulder, his touch was icy death and she did not want to feel it any longer. She spun around on her knees, knocking his hand off her shoulder and looked up at…it wasn't Hank. It wasn't even a person. She would never reconcile her rational mind with what it was she saw, what it was that spoke to her.

She did a double take at the apparition before her. It appeared much as a man from the late twentieth century. He even wore a Pearl Jam t-shirt. Other than that he was completely transparent and shone with an unearthly bluish light that mesmerized and sickened Amanda at the same time. She tried to scream, she tried to stand, she tried to move in any way at all and found that she could not. She was completely frozen with fear.

The spirit swam through the air, coming to rest mere inches from her face, letting out a low guttural growl. Amanda began to whimper but still found herself frozen stiff as her body refused to act as her mind recoiled in woeful terror. It fixed its hollow gaze upon her eyes and she became transfixed as if by some sort of hellish glamour.

"Do not be afraid dear thing. You have called me forth from my prison of dust and solitude. I mean you no harm. That was my typewriter, some twenty years ago," his voice was hollow and sounded like it was coming from a deep well and not right in front of Amanda.

"I…I didn't mean to do anything…I'm so sorry," she stammered as she spoke, trying to remain calm. She had never experienced anything even remotely similar and she had no baseline from which to judge a supernatural experience. Amanda didn't even fully believe that it was happening.

"Don't worry about me. I am more free than I have been in years. I was murdered in this house and I come with a message for you; if it is indeed you who lives in this house," he waited for her to confirm what he was saying before continuing.

"No, I am just visiting. Hank…he's out in the garage. He… he's a…a glassblower," she didn't know what to say to the ghost.

"Tell him to leave this place if he values his soul. This house will eat him alive and turn him into a thrall of the worm. We are all its servants, us ghosts of this house. We are all its slaves. There is no saving me, no saving the preacher or the hippies who lived here in the sixties. There's no saving the soldier and there's no saving the railwayman. He owns us all and he will own Hank too. Tell him!" the ghost trailed off and disappeared in a flash, flying into the typewriter in a ball of blue light. The smell of sulfur and ozone hung thick in the air.

Amanda could not believe what had just happened. She put a new sheet of paper in the typewriter and typed out everything the ghost had said to her to the best of her ability to remember.

After she was done she took the sheet out of the typewriter, folded it up and put it in her pocket as she went back downstairs, still shaken by what she went through. She was still cold and shaking from it but was also sweating and having hot flashes. Amanda stopped halfway down the steps and took several deep breaths, not continuing until she was done feeling weird and her head was clear.

"There must be some rational, scientific explanation for what just happened", she said aloud as she got to the bottom of the stairs. Amanda was sure that she had taken a nap while upstairs and it was a dream. No, that only lasted a moment. She wasn't capable of lying to herself that blatantly. She had to wrap her delusions in a blanket of complexity in order to baffle herself; she knew that is how her brain worked. What had just happened to her was beyond her ability to explain and it was beyond anything she had ever experienced. Still, that didn't mean that it was without explanation. Even if she never figured it out Amanda knew there was a way to explain her experience rooted in science. Had she snapped? No, she was sure that she was fine after she got downstairs. Maybe there was a gas leak, the house was really old.

As she considered all the options that came to mind Hank and Lief came inside, hurriedly and noisily. Hank was screaming and Amanda ran to the back door where they were coming in. She met them in the kitchen to see that Hank was holding his hand under cold water in the sink. He had obviously burned himself in the glass shop.

Lief saw Amanda standing there, in shock and staring. "He had a seizure at the bench and his hand went right into the torch. I was able to turn the damn torch off, or else he would've fallen right into the flame. He also dropped molten glass right on his seat. It damn near melted his dick off. Left a big ole hole in his office chair that he sits in at the workstation. It was insane. I'm just glad I was there. He still seems a little out of it," Lief let her know how severe it all was with the panicked tone he used.

After Hank ran his hand under the sink for a half an hour they put salve and gauze on the burns. He took several painkillers and without even thinking about Amanda went into his room, got out his rig and his dope and cooked himself up a spoonful of heroin. Amanda walked in right as he was spiking his vein and pushing in the plunger. As the drug hit him and he fell into bliss and calm he was a bit happy to see that she was not appalled at all. Amanda took the needle from him as he fell into a nod. She untied the rubber hosing he was using from his arm and tied herself off. Taking his rig and his dope off of the nightstand, where unbeknownst to them both Ana Sophia had grasped the scissors from that she would stab Yuri with, Amanda cooked up a shot of her own. She spiked her vein with his needle and shot heroin for the first time in fifteen years.

They spent the rest of the evening shooting heroin and fucking. Hank didn't know that she had been a junkie and that she had spent twelve years in recovery, but as they got high together he heard the entire tragic story of her life. He was shocked to find out that she had gone through college as a heroin addict. Still, it helped put the fact that she was still stripping into perspective for Hank. But even as the thoughts crossed his mind he felt as if he were being too judgmental of her. Who was he to judge anyone? She had a master's degree in microbiology. He was a simple weed grower. Even his own grandmother could take a cutting off of a plant and clone it. Suddenly he felt bad and confessed everything he was thinking to Amanda. To his surprise, she didn't care.

Instead, she found it to be endearing. After they both came out of a deep nod, drifting away on a sea of heroin bliss and feeling closer to him than she had yet, she confessed her experience in the upstairs to him. She thought they were on a level where they could tell each other anything, but he went ballistic, even as high as he was oh heroin, pills, and cannabis.

He ran upstairs in a panic, screaming incoherently about not touching anything in the room of antiques. She was able to derive that the items in the room had all belonged to former tenants but he was up the stairs before she could make out much else.

Amanda got to the top of the stairs and noticed that Hank was in the other room already and was swearing up a storm. She stood in the threshold and saw that he was hanging the tie-dye back up, but was shocked to see that there was no doll in the wheelchair. He put all the paperback in the desk and took her page out of the typewriter. Without even looking at what she had written he put the page and all the others in the drawer with the empty sheets. He then stood up and exited the room, walking right up to her as he pulled the door closed behind him.

"Now what was it that he said to you again Amanda?" Hank asked impatiently and she could tell that he felt the situation was dire.

"Hank you don't believe that there was really a ghost in here do you sweetie?" she asked him in a way that he immediately identified as condescending, even though he was so high that the world seemed like a fantasy.

"I don't know what I believe anymore Amanda. I just know that I'm crazy if I believe what has happened since I moved into this house. And if I don't believe it, well then I am having major hallucinations. One thing that I think is interesting is that you saw the doll...that thing...well, I'll tell you about it some other time. But you say you saw and talked to the ghost of a writer. I haven't met that one yet, but you also said that he mentioned the hippies and the preacher and the railwayman. I know the railwayman. Sometimes I can hear him and he talks to me," he opened up a little too much, he could tell she wasn't buying it.

"Hank I'm a scientist. I am a rationally minded person. I believe in the scientific method. None of this makes sense, but there is a good explanation for it. It might just be hard to see since we are in the middle of it. I want to believe you, I really do, but there just has to be a normal explanation for this shit," Amanda said as she could see that her logic was getting through to him.

He gave up the fight, not wanting to argue and seeing that he wasn't going to convince her either way. Hell, he hadn't even convinced himself. He knew he was totally crazy, but it was beginning to seem like way too much that both Amy and Amanda both talked to ghosts in the upstairs. He had never mentioned Larvamog to Amanda and for her to tell him that a ghost in his house sent him a warning about "the worm" seemed way too close to Hank's own personal insanity to suit him. The option that the Great Old One was indeed real, and had chosen his house as its residence, began to cross his mind again.

Hank was more confused than ever. He didn't know if he was living in a dream or dreaming in reality. He only knew that between the heroin and Amanda he was feeling great and didn't want to mess it up in any way. He suggested they leave the ghosts be and got back to living their own actual lives. As a way to celebrate their experiences, they decided to watch one of Hank's many horror DVD's.

When they got downstairs they made some microwave popcorn and coffee to drink. They rolled up some joints and both injected another load of Hank's dope. Curling up on the couch the two invited Lief out to the living room to watch the B-movie Dead Alive with them but he was too beat by the long day and just wanted to hit the hay. After some time, about halfway through the movie, they could hear the loud sound of Lief snoring in the other room.

Hank and Amanda laughed their way through the gory nineteen eighties horror comedy. It had much more gore than most movies in the genre and it made for a great time. As Hank sat on the couch, watching one of his favorite movies with a woman he'd fantasized about for twenty years or more and high as he could be he realized that he was truly happy. For the first time in years, he was a happy man. For the first time in years, he felt like he deserved to be a happy man.

As all of those revelations set in Hank heard the all too familiar voice of Quan Fong cutting through the air. He could tell that Amanda did not hear him.

"When you gonna tell her 'bout me, Hank? When you gonna tell her 'bout ole Quan?" the spirit taunted him.

Hank breathed in through his nostrils deeply, showing his annoyance to Quan, who he could not see.

"When you gonna tell her it was me fuckin' her wit' your dick Hank?" Quan's words cut Hank's ego like a knife cuts butter.

During one of the darker scenes in the movie, Hank dared to let a tear fall down his cheek, thankful that Amanda did not see it. He knew that his mind was shattered and that he had his own demons, but Quan taunting him was more than he could take in the wake of the revelations he was having concerning Amanda's experience.

Hank awoke the next afternoon on the couch to find a note telling him that Lief had given Amanda a ride back to Lexington. She had tried for a half hour to wake him up and say goodbye to him, to no avail, but would be looking forward to seeing him. Hank lit his morning cigarette and before he even made his coffee he went for his syringe. He shot half a load that was still in the needle. It gave him a slight high, but he craved more; needed more. Frantically he looked about for his heroin. It was gone. There wasn't a bit of dope in the entire house. He tore apart it from top to bottom. When the realization set in that Amanda had taken it he looked through his weed and his pills and his money as well.

She had hit him on all fronts. Every single dollar that he had, except what was in his private safe. She got at least five thousand dollars. She got hundreds of pills, only leaving his seizure meds and a single bottle of Valium.

"Fucking strippers," he muttered to himself under his breath, feeling betrayed and on top of that stupid for not having seen it coming a mile away.

THE VICTIMS AND THE WARRIORS

*H*ank had no luck in tracking down Amanda Wexler. He couldn't find an address for her and she had quit her job at Pure Gold. He figured that she probably just left town, she sure had enough money and drugs to make it happen. She was probably on a bus halfway to California. Hank was hurt by her actions but felt bad for Lief who had driven her all the way to Lexington and didn't even know that she had ripped them off. Lief seemed to take it pretty hard and felt like the whole situation was his own fault, even though Hank often reminded him that she was just a "scandalous ho."

Still looking for Amanda gave Hank a reason to go to Lexington; to go to strip clubs. He had no problem with that. After a month of frequenting a club called Solid Platinum, Hank became quite the regular and everyone loved it when he walked in. He'd often tip the doorman and the bartenders in marijuana. He was always low key about giving it to them, so as not to raise suspicion. That got him a certain celebrity status that had benefits far beyond knowing that doorman or getting hooked up on drinks. When word spread that Hank was the guy with all the good weed he was neck deep in strippers throwing themselves at him for a taste of his wares. It soon became common for Hank to go with a girl or two back to their place, although he had learned his lesson when he brought Amanda back to Gravel Switch. No more strippers would ever come back with him again, that was his new rule for himself and he didn't find it hard to follow.

One night, after spending the evening with a young woman from Indiana and shooting heroin, Hank dozed off at the wheel on the way home. He remembered waking suddenly, a loud crashing sound like the world exploding and metal wrenching apart. He remembered crawling out of the window of his over-turned Jeep Cherokee, he remembered there was blood all over him and he remembered the blackness taking him.

When he awoke he was in UK hospital, lying in a bed, hooked up to machines that monitored his vitals. It took him a while to open his eyes and as he did he could tell that his face was bruised up pretty badly. As his head swam from pain and painkillers, Hank found his first coherent thought to be about the irony of wrecking his Jeep from nodding out when he had always been paranoid that he would wreck while having a seizure.

He cleared his throat. Then he heard Amy's voice, soothing a calm.

"Hey there. How you feelin', Hank? You had a pretty bad wreck, we weren't too sure that you were gonna make it at first. Doctors were worried, but you pulled through. Can you talk?" she had been sitting in a chair next to his bed. After she spoke she leaned over and kissed him on the forehead. It felt amazing to Hank, but when he smiled it stung his still bruised face.

"I don't know what happened. I was driving, then I was

covered in blood. I dunno…" Hank seemed concerned, as if he needed to correct something. It was then that he saw that he was handcuffed to the bed.

"You were placed under arrest for possession of heroin. I already talked to Daniel," Amy spoke openly of the DEA officer who had been assigned their case in two thousand and three after they were busted in Danville for the cultivation of cannabis. They had a rocky relationship with Agent Daniel McCormick, but he did get them out of several pinches in their time. Always for a price and seldom one that they were truly willing to pay. It had never bothered Amy that they had become informants, but it ate away at Hank every day. When they made the deal to turn in the people they were working with, in exchange for their freedom, Hank had thought that he was willing to do anything to protect his marriage, to keep himself and Amy out of prison. What Agent McCormick had called on them to do, all the people they had sent to prison…it was something Hank tried to avoid thinking about at all costs.

"What do I have to do for Danny boy this time Amy? Oh, yeah, why are you here? Didn't we split up?" Hank got immediately irritated and afraid of what he was going to have to do. With all the people he had snitched on, he figured that he would be used to it but it never got any easier. Especially after he sent his friend Andrew to prison for ten years for growing cannabis. Even that wasn't enough for Agent McCormick who had demanded Hank and Amy set up several more of their friends, even wearing a wire on one occasion.

"He said that he owed us one, that we've been put through the ringer, but he will be in contact if he needs anything. Somebody should be here to uncuff you as soon as I call him back to let him know that you are awake now. As far as me and you… well, I've been thinking about it Hank and we have a lot to talk about. A big part of me knows I made a mistake and wants to come back, I know it was wrong of me to put Boris's death on you. Another part of me wants you back in my life, even if you only want to be friends. I miss you on more levels than just marriage. And as to that…well, they called me first when you came to the hospital because I am still your wife. We never filed for divorce so…" she broke off, staring away, averting her eyes and fearing his rejection.

"I love you, Amy. I missed you every moment of every day. I will do anything to get you back," he had no reason to lie, nor was he feeling good enough to put up a front.

"I love you too Hank. I love you too," she began to sob.

"What's wrong baby?" he asked concerned, he knew something else was bothering her.

"You are in liver failure. You can't handle all of the prescription pills you have been taking, even your seizure meds are too much. You have Hepatitis-C, it has been eating away at your liver for twenty years and now it's failing," she burst into full-on tears, still sobbing heavily.

"I had Hep-A back twenty years ago, but I got well. I was in the hospital for a while but I came out fine," he told her plainly and firmly as if it could change his diagnosis.

"The doctor said he's sure of it. Back then they misdiagnosed Hep-C as Hep-A a lot. I'm sorry Hank. I'm so sorry. There's things we can do, but if you don't take care of yourself and if you keep taking all of those pills, and shooting FUCKING HEROIN, then you won't live much longer baby," she wiped the tears away, determined to be uplifting for Hank, not depressing.

"Wow. I guess I will have to change everything," he thought about Amanda Wexler when he spoke, realizing that he had shared a needle with her and that she probably had Hep-C because of it. He was shocked that the thought didn't amuse him, especially after she had screwed him over so badly.

"Did I lose my license?" Hank asked Amy but he already knew the answer. She simply nodded in affirmation.

"Hank I have a lot to tell you about the house, the town, the people down there…there's a lot to it, a lot," she got excited, almost heated like she did when she was stressed out or even in danger.

"Tell me. Looks like we'll be here for a while."

"I went to the state records building in Frankfort, out by the state capitol. I looked at every record on file for Gravel Switch that I could find. Also lots about Bradfordsville and Marion County in general. Anyways, I learned a lot about the house. Hank…everyone that moves into that damn house dies. The last four tenants before us were all found dead on the property. Almost like clockwork, every twenty years or so. All dead by hanging and ruled a suicide but one, who was obviously killed by some sort of animal…probably one of the things that attacked me. I mean, Hank, this ain't coincidence. Before us, there was a writer who hung himself. Before him, there was a group of hippies in the sixties…" she trailed off again, spacing out as if a little too scrambled by the weight of it all to go on.

Hank laid his hand on her arm in reassurance and nodded for her to go on. She took a deep breath. Then she leaned in and hugged him. She took his head in her hands, gently so as not to hurt him, then showered his cheeks and lips with tender kisses. He felt alive and amazed that she was back in his life. Every bit of her affection did wonders to lift his spirits.

Amy continued after kissing Hank for a few minutes, "The hippies were having a party with some friends and several people disappeared, some were found naked and mutilated. One skinned completely alive. The father was found in the house, hung. There were several dead but also several survivors and they all said that the whole group had been abducted by aliens. It is a famous alien abduction story and that is why the writer moved in, he wanted to live in the house because he was writing a science fiction story based on the Gravel Switch abduction and massacre."

"My god. The damn house is a death trap," Hank could see that Amy needed a moment so he thought that he would interject.

"Yeah. It is. Okay, before the hippies there was a World War Two vet who came back and lived in the house. He was accused of killing a local boy and before he could go to trial hung himself in the house. Before him, was a preacher who killed his whole family and hung himself. The messed up thing is they were all ruled as suicide. Now it gets even better..." something in Amy's tone reminded Hank of a conspiracy theorist, but he was following her story without any problems.

"The house has been owned by the Hickman family the whole time, since nineteen hundred and five. Before that, it was owned by a Chinese railroad worker who came back east after completing the trans-continental railroad. Gravel Switch is where they quarried a bunch of the gravel for the railroads," Amy paused to breathe deeply.

"Quan. I know exactly who that motherfucker is," Hank was visibly pissed off at hearing the story of the railroad worker.

"Yes. Quan had raped his own daughter, whose mother was a Hickman. He was drunk one night after she realized that she was pregnant and he stabbed her to death with a pitchfork. When he sobered up he hung himself. The weird thing is all these hangings have been ruled suicide. But Hank, the local sheriff, and coroner...both offices, have been held by a member of the Hickman family or a cousin for over a hundred and fifty years. Bernice is one of the last with the name, Jared, too, but everyone in that damn town is related whether they will admit to it or not."

"My god. We don't stand a chance. What are they doing killing all these people? I mean, what is it all for?" Hank began to tremble a bit.

"They are in a cult Hank. They're called the Cult of the Black Goat. I know it sounds weird and I know that a lot of messed up shit has happened that we couldn't explain. But the truth is that thing you saw in the basement, that demon...the thing that attacked me in the field between the road and the house...all the spirits of the house, which I am convinced are all the dead previous tenants, Hank...they are all connected. And all the people in that damn town and surrounding area are working together somehow. I know I sound crazy as hell, but they are a cult and I know it. I know it, Hank, because Jared tried to induct me into it, or initiate or whatever it was he called it. Initiation. Jared is like some sort of high priest Hank. I played along for a while and learned about it all. The whole thing, the weed they grow, the Cornbread Mafia, all of it is Jared's. He controls everything and it is all a front to cover up the cult. They think they are going to open a gateway that lets demons into our reality and that if they do that then they will be spared and given wealth and power. The whole thing sounds like a bunch of Scientology to me. I mean it is weird, but they believe our house is built on the spot where the thing they are trying to summon will come through to our dimension. Jared even admitted that he was the one who shot Phyllis and that she was a sacrifice to the demon," she had much more to say but gave Hank a moment to respond.

"So Jared doesn't work for Alan then. Alan works for Jared.

Damn, they are slick. I can't believe that fucker. I'm sorry, I know you were dating him. Still, I always trusted him, didn't even mind when I knew he was fucking you. That isn't even like me. It was like I was his puppet that he just fed pills to. I was in such a daze that I didn't even seem to notice," Hank felt used and it was obvious on his face.

"Hank, we need to take Jared out before he does the same to us. It didn't go over too well that I didn't want to join their cult. I mean I was actually going to join until I found out about the human sacrifice. I mean, my friggin' god, you know?" she had a look of disgust on her face like she had stepped in dog poop and had to scrape it off of her shoe.

"Yeah. We really do. He's too dangerous and obviously thinks that we are some kind of victims. Fuck him. I'll shoot that fucker in the goddamn face!" Hank got loud enough that a nurse poked her head in to check on them but Amy waved her off, letting her know everything was alright with a smile.

Hank was glad to ride home the next day with Amy. It felt right to be riding in her car again. It felt right to have her next to him, to hear her voice, to kiss her and to hold her. Hank was looking forward to popping a Viagra when they got back to Gravel Switch, though he planned to surprise her with it. He did know that it would be awkward to explain to her that he had put all of her things in the shacks out back where Sheridan and Matilda had once lived a hundred and fifty years before. Still, it wasn't anything to stress on and he would cross that bridge when he came to it.

He explained Lief and everything the young man did for him and Amy seemed fine with the idea of having another person live with them. The house was certainly big enough for three people and she expressed that she would feel safer with a third person there. Especially after her falling out with Jared.

She feared that he would come by with some of his cronies and try to cause trouble for her, especially once he figured out that she was back with Hank.

When they got back to the house Amy rolled up a joint and Hank went upstairs to get Lief who was checking the pH of the water in the hydroponic reservoir. By the time they came downstairs Amy had rolled and lit the joint and hit it a few times.

"You must be Lief, nice to meet you!" she said in a bubbly voice that was the only speech she could manage as she had taken too big a hit off of the joint and was stifling a cough.

He reached out and shook her hand. "Nice to meet you to Amy. Glad to finally put a face to the name."

The three of them sat and smoked weed together for hours. They put the satellite radio channel on the Grateful Dead and just chilled and talked. Eventually, Lief revealed that he had been experiencing supernatural events ever since he had moved in but had been afraid to talk about it. After seeing him open up and after seeing how obviously uncomfortable it made him they told him everything, from Jared to Larvamog. They wanted him to know what he was up against and more so they wanted to inform him of what they thought they were all up against.

He seemed to take it all in much more easily than either of them thought he would. After Hank had finished the entirety of the tale and explained the depth of their desperation to see an end to it all he was quite happy that his apprentice came on board as a full on soldier in the fight.

"How do we kick their ass?" was the first thing the younger man asked, followed by some hard punches thrown into his own hand.

"We don't know yet. God, I wish Phyllis was still with us. But when we figure it out we will not hesitate to take the fight to them. As far as I'm concerned their cult can suck it, their demon-thing…maggot, whatever…can suck it too. This is our house! If they are trying to bring demons into the world through our house, then we need to fuck them up!" Amy was feeling angry and ready to take the fight to them. It made Hank wonder exactly what it was that she had gone through with Jared.

Hank was relieved to see that Lief and Amy got along so perfectly. It made the strange transition smooth for everyone. The next few weeks were great for them all. Hank's liver enzymes tested poorly and his skin started to turn a bit grey, his eyes began to yellow with jaundice but all of that seemed secondary to the spiritual fight that they were all engaged in together. They felt stronger as a unit and spent much time together trying to contact the spirits of the house via an Ouija board but were repeatedly unsuccessful. The house seemed to know that they were rallying against the dark side, against the demons and their servants in Gravel Switch.

All three of them seemed to agree that Hank would not get his health under control until they were able to cleanse the house and stop the cult from bringing its plans to fruition. It was that line of thinking that prompted Lief to take decisive action and arm the group. He went to the Wal-Mart in Danville and bought two double barrel twelve gauge shotguns, one for Hank and one for Amy, and a thirty-eight caliber revolver for himself. Hank and Amy were both glad to get a shotgun and wondered why they had never considered arming themselves before. It made them do some thinking about how their hippie lifestyle had come at the expense of some basic survival skills.

They went out in the field and practiced shooting every day. All three of them became adequate marksmen in little time.

They even had the joy of seeing Alan drive by one day and stop in the road to observe them gunning down some targets they had attached to hay bails. Hank still intended to pay Alan the last two thousand clones he owed but he had put little more than zero effort into it in months. He really no longer cared if Alan got paid, but because he considered himself a man of his word he intended to pay. As far as Alan owning him, well Alan could suck his double barrel. Hank had had enough of the Cornbread Mafia and their bullshit. He often joked to himself that they were just some kind of Satanic, Redneck, Inbred, Hillbilly branch of Scientologists and he wouldn't be bullied or harassed by them ever again.

18

THE CROWN

The day after Alan saw Hank, Amy and Lief in the field shooting guns Hank called Alan up on the phone to let him know that it would still be a while before he could do another two thousand clones. It was true, his mother plant could not have any more branches cut off of her. He did not want to stress his mother, so he passed the news on to Alan, giving him as much head's up as possible that the clones would be delayed yet again. He neither knew nor cared how the country boy took the news. Hank felt free of the shackles the Cornbread Mafia had been restraining him with. He was unaware that all of that confidence had only come to him after acquiring a firearm and learning how to properly use it.

He went to bed early that night, leaving Lief in the garage to blow glass and Amy was at work so an early night didn't seem so bad to him. He fell into a deep sleep and relaxed a little more than he had in many months, other than the first few days when Amy had come back or that night he spent with Amanda Wexler. It was strange to him that he heard nothing at all as he woke up, tossing and turning from a nightmare to find a figure in all black standing over him. He heard the all too familiar sound of a shotgun being cocked and was told by a deep and gruff voice to, "Get up."

Hank got out of bed and the man told him to get dressed and to come outside with him. Hank had never been a hostage before, other than Quan's, and he did everything the man asked without hesitation. When he got outside he saw Lief was unconscious on the front porch, knocked out cold with a small trickle of blood coming from a dent in his forehead that would surely be needing stitches. The moon was full and Hank could make out that much, enough to know that Lief would probably be alright. When they got out to the yard he could make out the shape of Alan's van. Shit! He was being taken to Alan.

He got in the back of the van and was surprised to see that Michael Williams was in the back of it as well. The only difference was that Michael was hog-tied and had a gag in his mouth. Hank was shocked to be told that he was riding shotgun. He had gotten in the back of the van but was being made to ride in the front. He was not sure what to make of the situation. Alan was at the wheel but didn't say a word, so neither did Hank. The man with the gun got in the back with Michael, kicking him in the stomach as he did so. Michael let out a yelp that was audible even through the gag.

It was a short drive to Alan's house and when they got there Alan finally spoke as he parked the van. "You get'ta see what happens to motherfuckers that don't follow the rules tonight Hank. You get'ta see what I'ze got in store for ya, buoy," Alan was not messing around. Hank could tell he was much angrier than he anticipated the man would be.

As Hank got out of the van the big man in all black got out of the back and kept the shotgun pointed at Hank as he marched him into Alan's backyard. Alan whistled loudly and several men came out of his house, some Hank recognized, some he did not. They went to the van and grabbed Michael up and carried him behind Hank and the man with the shotgun.

"Michael, we gonna feed ya to the coyotes!" Alan yelled at Michael but Hank knew the words were meant for him as well.

When they were all gathered in the backyard Hank noticed that everything was pretty well visible because of the light of the full moon. The yard seemed empty. He wondered what it was that was going to happen, were they going to shoot Michael?

His question was quickly answered and all the men who carried Michael out of the van took him to a spot in the middle of the yard. They laid him on the ground and there were stakes on the ground that Hank could not see until they began to tie him to them with a rope that one of the men had carried over his shoulder. Another man, one that Hank recognized as the bet taker at the dogfight where Boris had died, produced a knife and they cut Michaels shirt open, then cut a deep gash across his stomach and chest. He screamed in agony. Hank could tell it was not a fatal wound, but it was definitely a world of pain.

The men all retired to the house, leaving Michael whimpering on the ground.

The man with the shotgun joined them, leaving Hank alone with Alan. Before Hank could speak Alan whistled again.

"Now we wait," the local man said.

Feeling as if he had nothing to lose Hank replied, "For What?"

But his question was answered much more quickly that he thought it would be as two red eyes appeared, attached to the head of a hulking black form that reminded Hank of a wolf. He couldn't tell where it had come from. It would have had to have walked a hundred yards across an open field to get to where they were, from any direction. Yet there it was, right atop Michael.

Hank could smell the thing, a cross between rotting cheese and sewage. He had never smelled anything so wretched, not even the maggot-thing Larvamog itself. He assumed that the beast was one of the cosmic worm's own terrible children. The spawn that could stalk the earth in bodies of flesh. He was not wrong.

Its head lolled back and forth inches above Michael, slathering thick ropes of a wretched saliva-like ooze across his face. It let out a noise that could have been a wolf's growl if it were coming through a megaphone. Just as Hank figured that it was indeed some sort of a mutant wolf a thick ropy tentacle appendage covered in suckers lashed out from its back and plunged into Michael's stomach. It made a sickening squelching sound and the gag did nothing to stifle Michael's cry of total suffering.

Then the thing began to pump life fluid through it, in strong gulps, making lumps of blood bubble up through the tentacle appendage as it drank Michael's life away. Hank turned to avert his eyes. There was a strong sulfur smell and a loud crack like thunder at ground level, then Hank could tell that the thing was gone.

Michael was still alive, though bleeding profusely. He whimpered and shuddered. Hank watched in terror as Alan walked over to Michael and stuck a large hunting knife into the wound in his stomach and opened him up from sternum to navel. Michael gave out one last scream as his back arched up from the ground he was staked to and his life force left his body for good. Alan got on his knees and began to pull Michael's intestines out by hand. He pulled out several feet of entrails and severed them off of the fresh corpse with the knife.

Hank closed his eyes, he didn't want to see such brutality. The gore was making him queasy and he thought that he would pass out. As he clenched his eyelids closed as tightly as he could an overwhelming anxiety overtook him. Then he felt the strong force of a blow to the face, across his right cheek. Hank dropped to his knees and before he could rise back up Alan had dumped several pounds of Michael's guts over his head. A crown of guts and gore, excrement spilling out of the intestines all over Hank's chest. He began to react, but before he could even move at all Alan put the hunting knife right into his face.

"This is the bed you made motherfucker. Now you're gonna lie in it bitch" Alan said in a spitting hiss, spraying Hank in the face with saliva as he spoke, though it mattered little. Hank was covered head, neck, shoulders, and chest with the blood, guts, and shit of Michael Williams.

The man with the shotgun came back outside and pointed it at the back of Hank's head. Alan demanded that he get back into the van. Hank did just as he was told, guts and all. He was too afraid to try to remove them again. As he walked he stopped for a moment to vomit and Alan laughed at him, a laugh of malicious pleasure.

Alan drove Hank back to his house and he was happy to see that Amy was already home. Hopefully, she would be able to help Lief and they would be armed and waiting when Alan returned. Hank was disappointed when Alan put him out of the truck at the same point where Amy had wrecked her car.

"Walk bitch. And do be careful," Alan said sarcastically. "There's monsters out here and you're covered with guts buoy."

Alan slammed the door and peeled out, leaving Hank alone in the moonlight, aware that something was watching him.

He flung the intestines off of his neck and ran as fast as he could back to the house. When he got halfway down the driveway he started yelling for Amy and Lief but it was a minute before either of them made it outside. He collapsed on the porch, still drenched in Michael's gore and fluids. He was in the midst of a full-blown grand mal seizure when they got to him.

19

THE FLOOD

*T*he traumatic events of the night before made quite an impression on the Ramsey's and Lief, who had only been knocked out and suffered a little swelling from the blow he took. The big man in black with the shotgun had hit him in the forehead with the butt of the gun, he hadn't even seen it coming. Hank recovered from his seizure and got himself cleaned up but was still quite shaken the next morning.

The three discussed what to do over breakfast. Revenge was on all their minds but it didn't seem to be a real option. How could they combat such forces? Hank's questions about his sanity and the experiences he had been having were all answered. He felt crazier than ever admitting to himself that they were all one hundred percent real. When Hank recollected the event that took the life of Michael Williams they all seemed to come to the same conclusion. Getting out of Gravel Switch and moving somewhere far, far away was the only option for survival. They all needed to disappear and adopt new identities. Lief agreed that he would move with them and change his name. The Pacific Northwest or the San Francisco Bay Area seemed to be the favorite choices. Amy had an uncle in Washington state up near the Canadian border and Hank had an old high school friend who lived in San Francisco. Lief didn't care much either way what they did. He just didn't want to get caught up in any of the violence that was sure to follow.

And just like that, over bacon and eggs, coffee and a joint in the morning the three of them decided that there was no fighting the cult, there was no cleansing the house, there was no survival unless they packed their bags up and left as soon as possible.

They spent the next couple of weeks packing up much of what they had into boxes. Hank was finally able to convince Amy that she was a hoarder and that they had accumulated a lot of junk since she had been working at Walgreen's. They threw out a lot of her junk and had a large bonfire in the back-yard one night and burned some furniture, clothes, and books that they no longer wanted. Hank dialed back his production of marijuana and had his final cycle planted in rockwool cubes. It was twenty-eight days out from harvest and then it had to dry. After that, they could move on and leave the nightmare that was Gravel Switch behind them. The future looked bright, brighter than it had when they had first decided to leave Lexington. Just over a month to go didn't seem like too daunting of a prospect considering all that they had been through.

Chris Wilson came to the house to help them pack. They were happy to see him and to get all the help they could get. Even though Hank had known Chris for most of his life he was not comfortable sharing the full extent of what they were going through. Chris could tell that something major was happening, but he gave them their privacy, for the most part, only inquiring where it was that they were going to move to.

Halfway through the day Hank took him aside and revealed that they would be disappearing. Changing identities and moving to the west coast were only part of it. Chris understood that it would be the last time that he saw his dear friend. They reminisced about old times, hanging out with Yuri and their other friends Kevin and Justin, who had moved to San Francisco in the nineties.

Chris rolled a joint up and took Hank out onto the front porch, sitting in a rocking chair he lit the joint and sighed deeply. They didn't speak much but they both knew it was the last joint that they would ever smoke together, which was something major for them both as their entire group of friends had all come together around their common love of marijuana back in high school. It was a bittersweet moment for them both. The end of an era.

Just as they got down to the roach the sun was setting out over the barn. They stood on the porch arms around each other's shoulders, two old friends taking in a beautiful sunset before parting ways forever. Their serene moment was shattered by Amy screaming at the top of her lungs, "Hank! Come quick! Hank! It's Lief! He's trapped in the bathroom. They won't let him out! He's being attacked!"

Hank ran into the house, followed by Chris. Amy was in the hallway banging on the bathroom door. Water was coming out from under the door and they could hear that the sink was running. Chris nudged Amy aside and threw his shoulder into the heavy oak door. It groaned under his weight but it took three more times and a fierce front kick to blast the door open. It splintered the door frame around the lock.

When they got the door open things were dire indeed. Lief

was lying on the floor with a needle still in his arm and his lips were blue and his skin pale, grayish-white. His eyes were rolled back in his head and his mouth was full of foam. As Chris and Hank got the apprentice out of the bathroom Amy slipped in and turned the water off. She knew that the flood in the bathroom would mess the floor up and the landlord would want to charge them to fix it, but she really didn't care. None of it mattered anymore anyway.

Hank and Chris got Lief to Chris's car and without even consulting Amy or taking the time to tell her what was happening they peeled out, spun the car around and blasted down the driveway on the way to the closest hospital. Chris drove like a madman and when they got to Danville Hank was surprised that they didn't get pulled over.

They got to the hospital and Chris pulled up into the emergency lane for ambulances. Hank jumped out and ran inside letting the first nurse he could find know that his friend was dying of an overdose in the car. Within a few seconds, a code blue alert was issued over the hospital's public address system and several personnel came running out of the hospital to the car.

Lief was pulled out of the car, strapped to a gurney and as they started wheeling him inside Hank stood still in shock unable to hear the questions that a doctor was asking him. Chris stepped in to answer for him as the gurney disappeared down a hallway and behind a door. The last thing Hank saw before Lief was gone from his sight was a nurse doing chest compressions and another strapping an oxygen bag to his face, trying their best to resuscitate the unfortunate young man.

Chris moved his car out of the emergency ambulance-only area after a sheriff came up and reminded him that he needed to or he would be ticketed. Hank found a seat in the waiting room and the weight of the situation came to bear down on him when he realized that he would have to call Mr. and Mrs. Gutsell and tell them their son had overdosed on heroin. Even if Lief survived it would be a horrible experience to tell them about it. He wondered if his life was nothing but sorrow and insanity.

Chris came back into the emergency room waiting area and sat with Hank. He wasn't there ten minutes before a doctor came out to see them. Before the man even spoke to them they could tell Lief was gone. Hank began to cry a steady stream of tears as the doctor's words hit ears that had heard enough bad news.

They had to stay at the hospital for several hours. Hank had a lot of questions to answer. Doctors, cops, ultimately Lief's parents would have to get an explanation. He left the job of delivering the bad news to the doctor. He didn't have the heart to tell the Gutsells that their son had died. The fact that he was only nineteen was what Hank kept fixating on. It seemed like such a horrible waste of potential, of life.

After several hours of questioning, the doctors and police officers let Hank and Chris go. There were so many heroin overdoses in Kentucky that it was not uncommon, even in Danville. Hank had been worried that the cops were going to want to come to his house and search it, ostensibly for Lief's dope. He was petrified that they would raid him, but the officer in charge set his mind at ease and assured him that they were just trying to get the story straight. Since they brought him into the hospital they could rule out foul play and if they went around raiding everyone who had a person overdose at their home they would spend a lot of time and effort, not to mention money, to little effect. Hank was shocked that he found a humanizing element in the officer.

The man behind the badge showed him compassion during his time of grief.

"Maybe it has something to do with being a small town cop?" Hank wondered.

Chris drove Hank back to Gravel Switch several hours later than he was supposed to be home. He was due back in Lexington at midnight and didn't leave the hospital in Danville until three in the morning. After getting Hank home he decided to crash out there and go back to Lexington in the morning. He had forgotten to call his wife during all of the commotion of tragedy. When he got back to Gravel Switch he called her first thing, seeing on his cell phone screen that she had left him several voice mail messages. When he got her on the line she began telling him off for not calling her, immediately launching into a manic tirade.

"Lief O.D.'ed. He's dead," as soon as Chris said the words she immediately shifted gears to a quiet calm.

"Oh," he could tell she was about to cry uncontrollably. "He's dead? Oh my god. Oh my god. I can't believe it." She hung up, not even letting him explain the situation. He didn't mind, Chris was glad to get off of the phone. He would have plenty of time to talk to her when he got back to Lexington. He just needed a few hours sleep before the two-hour drive.

20

THE THRESHOLD

*T*he day after Lief died Hank decided that he and Amy had enough money and marijuana that they could leave. Hank didn't care to stay another few weeks to finish growing his last few plants and Amy supported him in that fully. He could take a loss, pull them prematurely. The buds wouldn't be sellable as they were but he planned to use them to produce a batch of hash oil, which he would still sell in the end, so it wasn't a total loss. The idea of just packing up and leaving everything behind made them both anxious. Hank and Amy had both been totally unaware that Lief was a heroin user. No wonder he had been so tolerant of Hank's drug abuse. They didn't want any more surprises.

Chris left not much after the sun was up. He had a cup of coffee with

Hank but wanted to be sober for the drive and so didn't smoke a morning bowl or joint with him. It was a sober departure after a long, deep hug. They had thought they said their final goodbyes the day before but then Lief had died and it sent everything into chaos again. The only conversation they had that morning was about chaos and being constantly thrown into the midst of it.

Hank stood on the porch as his friend drove away. He watched him all the way down the driveway and down the road until Chris was out of sight. Hank went inside to get Amy up. It was time to pack the last of their things, cut the last of the plants down, break down the grow room and finally to give the key to the landlord.

They could both see freedom ahead, could taste the crossing of the finish line that was their race against Gravel Switch. It was something they had been dreaming about, talking about, putting all their energy towards. As they got the last of their things together and into boxes, Hank realized that it was going to take him all night to break down his grow equipment. He had a hundred plants, all about two feet tall, and all the hydroponic equipment to deal with; as well as his nutrients and lighting, his reservoir and all of his pH balancing solutions. Amy encouraged him not to just abandon it all as it could be evidence that could be used against them. She was very uncomfortable leaving the grow equipment, even if they did take the plants. Anything they left could come back and bite them later, especially if something went wrong with their move to the west coast. The logic was hard for Hank to argue with.

Knowing they would be spending another night in the house Hank took his time breaking everything down. It was his intention to set up another grow room wherever they went and both California and Washington had legalized cannabis for medicinal use. With his epilepsy, he was certain to get a medical marijuana recommendation from any doctor he saw. Amy went to bed before he was even done cutting all the plants down. He decided to dry them at least overnight and strung some string from wall to wall and hung the freshly cut, premature plants. He was just finishing when he heard the distinct sound of a shotgun blast ringing through his house followed by the sound of Amy's voice screaming.

"Hank! Help! Hank!" she sounded absolutely frantic.

Hank ran to the steps and slipped on the way down, falling down half of the stairs on his butt, hitting the ground feet first and running into the bedroom where Amy had been. He saw the big man with the black ski mask and the shotgun again. Amy was in front of him on her knees with her hands behind her head. Hank panicked. He realized the man with the gun was between him and his own weapon. Amy's was with Hank's, on the far side of the bedroom, on the other side of the bed it may as well have been a mile away.

Hank stood in the doorway to his bedroom, gasping for air, looking at his wife as she cried. A hand came to rest on Hank's shoulder from behind. He jumped with fear and spun around to see Alan standing there. Alan shoved a pistol right into Hank's stomach, making him double over. The local man motioned for Hank to go into his room. Alan put Hank on his knees next to Amy and held the barrel of the thirty-eight to his forehead.

Hank closed his eyes and waited for what seemed like an eternity but no shot came. Alan had lifted the gun and holstered it. He grabbed Hank under the arm and jerked him to his feet so hard that Hank knew he would have a bruised armpit. Alan motioned for Amy to get to her feet as well.

The man with the shotgun marched them through the house, out the front door onto the porch. Alan followed close behind and closed the front door behind him. When they got to the porch the couple were amazed to see that dozens of people had gathered in their front yard. There was a large bonfire lit and everyone there was garbed in a black robe with a hood that covered them from head to toe. A few of the robed figures closest to the porch had a thick white stripe down their robes that ran the length of the front and over the hood, making them look much like skunks.

The man with the shotgun went out into the crowd and disappeared. Alan still stood behind Hank and Amy.

He put the gun to Amy's temple and said, "Take off all of your clothes, both of you." He was so direct and cold that neither of them hesitated in the slightest. They both stripped bare naked.

Hank covered his genitals with his hands but Amy stood defiant. They were both trembling in fear. Neither of them had ever seen anything like the throng gathered in their yard. The severity of the situation was not lost on them. Several of the congregants lit tiki torches off of the bonfire and made a path that was wide enough for two people to walk abreast from the porch to the bonfire. Hank let out a little urine as he struggled to contain his fear. They were both shaking from the cold fall air. They both noticed Kelly Williams and D.E.A. agent Daniel McCormick among the congregation of maniacs.

"Come forth high priest!" Alan yelled out to the crowd.

A figure in a black robe with a red stripe, much like the white ones, emerged from deep within the crowd and there was a steady chattering of teeth clicking together as he walked to the porch. He carried a plain black robe in his hands. When he got to the porch he walked right between Hank and Amy straight to Alan. They could see that the figure was Jared. He gave the robe to Alan, who put it on over his regular clothes. It had a yellow stripe down the front and on the hood, then all the way down the back. It occurred to Hank that their cult was much more organized than he had ever imagined.

As Alan got robed Jared pulled out a large, curved ritual blade from under his robe. He walked between Hank and Amy, to the front of the porch, caressing Amy's ass with the blade of his sacrificial knife. He addressed the crowd by lifting his hand in the air and giving a strange sign, a gesture neither Hank nor Amy had ever seen before. He followed it with a series of deliberate slashes through the air. When he was done he took a step back and the crowd roared.

"S'arl Amoth! Ia Shub-Niggurath!" They were words Hank had never heard before, but he knew they meant he and his wife were screwed. Amy had seen the words at Jared's house once, scrawled on a piece of paper. When she had asked about what it was he had told her that it was from a religious studies class he had taken in college and that it was a phrase from a dead language that hadn't been spoken for thousands of years. At the time she seemed content with the answer. At the moment she wished that she had found out more, but he had gotten irritated just at the mention of it so she had let it go.

Jared turned back toward Hank and Amy. Alan cleared his throat to remind them both that he was still present in case either of them tried to flee. Not that there was anywhere to go except empty fields until they got to woods, which the locals knew much better than they did. Hank had never felt so much like a fish out of water. He knew he was about to be ritually sacrificed. He looked over at his wife and stared deep into her eyes. "I love you Amy," was all he could say. She gave him the best Mona Lisa smile that she could manage, trying to reassure him. Trying to be supportive even in such a moment of pure terror. Jared grabbed her by the wrist and dragged her forcefully down the stairs and started pulling her toward the bonfire. Alan kicked Hank in the lower back and he fell straight to the ground, skinning his knee on the pavement of the walkway from the front porch to the driveway, leaving a thick, bloody smear that he could easily see in the torchlight.

Alan dragged Hank to his feet and grabbed him by the hair, put the gun to his head and marched him to the fire right behind Amy and Jared. The entire crowd's focus shifted from the porch to the fire. When Hank got there he saw that they were fitting Amy with a black robe, but it had a white sash tied around the waist. She seemed confused and he saw tears flowing down her cheek in the firelight. A random, robed figure brought forth a goat, leashed with a simple rope.

Jared shouted the strange phrases again, followed by several other more guttural noises that Hank couldn't follow. Noises that did not come from any human language and reminded Hank of a cat hacking up a fur ball more than any spoken tongue. He was floored when the crowd would return Jared's strange calls. Jared pointed the blade at the goat and it shone brightly in the firelight.

As he raised the blade Hank followed it and noticed Jared had it pointed at the full moon. He turned toward Hank and leaned in close to him and whispered in his ear, "Tonight is the full moon. Tonight all the gas giants are in conjunction. Jupiter, Saturn, Uranus, and Neptune. This night has been millennia in coming. This night we bring our Lord to this world. This night we make our lord flesh and you have the privilege, out of everyone in all of humanity to be the offering that calls him forth. A new era will come and the world will know the power of the Old Ones. You should rejoice. It is your blood that has been chosen."

Hank began to cry. Jared turned back to the goat and slit its throat. He took a handful of its hot blood and wiped it on Amy's face, chanting in that strange tongue. He shouted something that sounded much like gibberish and the crowd returned something equally as ridiculous sounding. Jared snapped his fingers and two men came forward and threw the body of the goat into the fire. When they were done they both knelt in front of Jared and tilted their heads all the way back after lowering their hoods. Their bare throats, exposed in the firelight and the full moon, were quickly turned crimson by Jared's blade. Hank and Amy both gasped as they again recognized their handler, agent McCormick as one of the two. The men had given themselves willingly, without hesitation. Pure cult fanaticism like they had never imagined. Jared put his empty hand to each of their throats and smeared a swath of blood across Amy's chest and breasts. She squirmed at his touch, as he put his hand beneath her robe and smeared her with the cultist's life essence. Four others came forward and threw the two bodies into the bonfire. The smell sickened Hank, not because it was foul, but because it reminded him of any other meat cooking and it made his stomach growl. He was appalled at his own body's natural reaction to cooking meat.

The people who had been nearest the porch, with the robes striped with white, came forward as a group. One of them had a satchel that appeared to be made out of human skin. They opened it up and Jared reached his hand into it and produced a powder that he threw into the fire, producing a bright green light that lasted for several seconds. "S'arl Amoth! S'arl Amoth Te Za'vrock! S'arl Amoth!" he shouted and the crowd repeated the same three times after him, sending chills through Hank and Amy both.

The second of the white striped figures produced something from under her robe and it took a moment for Hank to see it as it was in shadow from his angle, but Amy immediately noticed that it was the severed head of an infant, retching as she beheld it her mouth filled with bile. Jared took the tiny head and raised it into the air. The crowd shouted something neither Hank nor Amy could make out and Jared threw it into the fire too. The fire roared, sparked and hissed. The flame itself then turned the shade of green it had previously but remained that color as the fire swelled into a thirty foot, roaring conflagration fueled by some eldritch and unknowable power.

Another of Jared's deacons stepped forward. This one pulled a living pit bull puppy out from under his robe. Jared just gave a gesture with his blade and the deacon tossed it right on the fire. Hank cried out, "You Fucker!" as he heard the poor animal shrieking in anguish as the flames consumed it. Alan's foot kicked him in the knee from behind and he fell to the ground with a thud, landing right on his bloodied kneecaps.

Hank stayed down for a moment, trying not to see any more of the horrors. After another few minutes of chanting and throwing things into the fire the cult, in unison, took a few steps back. Hank and Amy joined them instinctively, fearing something might emerge from the fire.

Several more minutes passed in what seemed like total silence. Then just as the Ramseys were both wondering what was about to happen, if anything, a thick, sickly yellow smoke came rolling out of the fire. It coalesced above the flames and they went out entirely, although it got brighter as the thick smoke became luminescent. A ghastly green glow filled the yard and the field and all the robed figures fell to their knees in prostration, touching their foreheads to the ground and chanting, "S'arl Amoth! S'arl Amoth!" Only Jared still stood, along with Hank and Amy.

The cloud of smoke began to coalesce and swirl about in a vortex that kicked up a high wind around the entire yard. It began to shine brighter by the moment, bathing everything in the wretched green light. Lightning began to crackle through it in arcing bursts. The smoke shot into the sky, a green pillar all the way to the clouds, it seemed almost solid. An amorphous face came together in the center of it, some thirty feet off of the ground. Two large red eyes the size of men opened in the face that was otherwise featureless. They slanted in a sinister, piercing gaze and a voice that was thunder and death rang out, addressing Jared directly.

"High priest. You have called me forth. It was not my time to entire your world. A thousand, thousand lifetimes will pass before I make myself whole in your realm. You dreamed of power and so you opened the gate, thinking I would come through the threshold and thrust it upon you. I offer only death."

Jared's deacons all stood up in unison as if receiving a message no one else could hear. They seized him, disarmed him and dragged him to the bonfire pit where the entity's disembodied spirit was hovering between worlds. Jared did not protest, he was totally silent. He was put on his knees.

"Hank, they thought that you were the chosen feast that I would dine on. That your soul should be the nourishment that I required to manifest. The fools! Come, plunge the blade into the heart of this priest and let his death have meaning where his life did not," the voice was more than Hank could resist. Even as it spoke he felt compelled to obey it, didn't even consider that there was another option.

It was only when he had the ritual knife in hand that he noticed the red eyes of the children of Larvamog all around, at the periphery of the yard, just out of the firelight. He would have never even known they were there if it weren't for their eyes. Then Hank stared Jared in the eyes deeply, showing no mercy with his own stare. Jared closed his eyes and began chanting to himself under his breath. Amy screamed as Hank brought the blade down in a brutal thrust. He plunged it into Jared's chest as deeply as he could and gouts of blood pumped out onto Hank's hand. He found pleasure in stabbing Jared so he did it again, and again, and again. He stabbed Jared until he could no longer stab because he lacked the strength to go on. He was no longer totally naked. Hank wore a suit of blood, nearly from head to toe.

Hank and the deacons, without even communicating, threw Jared's body on the smoldering embers as the sky-high pillar of glowing green smoke dissipated, lightning arcs crackling as it did so.

Hank didn't even care what was going to happen next. He turned to see Amy was only a few feet behind him and that all of the cult members were standing again, mulling about, wondering what just happened and what to do about it. Hank grabbed Amy's hand and they began running for the house as fast as they could while the cult was still confused. Hank had picked the ritual knife up again after throwing Jared in the fire and he used it to hack at anyone that came between them and getting back inside and to their shotguns.

There was the loud sound of gunshots and the screams of somebody getting shot, mixed with the screams of a few men Hank had severely wounded with the knife. As they got to the front door and made it back inside the house, Hank noticed Alan standing in the middle of the yard, pointing his pistol at the house. The glass pane in the window of the front door exploded as a bullet came through right next to Hank's head. He turned to run back further into the house and noticed that Amy had already gotten their shotguns out of the bedroom and was heading back to the foyer to shoot anybody that approached the front door.

She threw Hank his shotgun and they both pointed out the

front door and started blasting. They took their time aiming, even hit a few of the cultists, but Alan was nowhere to be seen. The remaining robed cult members scrambled out of the yard, all to vehicles which had been parked out on the main road. Hank and Amy kept firing until they no longer saw nor heard anything else.

Hank didn't even wash the gore and blood off of his naked body until the sun had risen. Still, he took his loaded shotgun into the bathroom with him and had Amy watching the approach to the front door, using binoculars to see anyone long before they even made it to the driveway. As he washed off his red suit Hank wondered how many dead bodies were in his front yard.

21

THE BATTERY

Hank got out of the shower and yelled through the house for Amy to make sure that everything was okay and that they hadn't come back in those few minutes. She affirmed that everything was fine. She was sitting on the porch smoking a cigarette. He dried off and went into the bedroom where they had the last of their things, other than the grow room in the upstairs and all the equipment. As far as he was concerned they were going to leave it all behind. After all, staying an extra day to clean up had resulted in the horrible events of the previous evening. Who knew what staying another day would cause? They had bigger problems than the grow room to worry about anyway. What about the bodies in the front yard? Some of them were sure to be victims of their own shotguns.

Hank decided that he might leave the lights and the hydroponic setup, but he wasn't going to leave the plants themselves hanging. He went upstairs to get them, taking an empty duffle bag with him to shove as many plants into as he could take with him. The majority would be left behind, he knew, but he would take what he could get and was determined not to make it a total loss.

As he got about halfway up the stairs he collapsed, feeling a deep pain in his side. Hank knew he wasn't having a seizure, but he knew over the past few days he hadn't taken his medications as he should. Trying to wean off of so many drugs in order to keep his dying liver from giving up on him was a good effort, but one enacted far too late. He knew that eventually, he would have to give up all of his drugs if he wanted treatment for his hepatitis. He just didn't expect that his liver would give him so many problems, he had been in a deep denial about the state of his health since he had been diagnosed with Hep-C and told his liver was failing.

Hank struggled to his feet, he told himself that he had to endure, had to press on. Every part of him just wanted to lay down and give up. He could tell that he was full of toxins, that his liver hadn't been doing its job in a long time. His own blood was poison, a vile venom that kept him in a delirium. Hank could feel a terrible headache come on as he realized that his brain was being poisoned by his own nasty blood. He fought to clear his mind, breathing deeply and trying to center himself.

After a few minutes, Hank was able to drag himself up to the top of the staircase, using the handrail to bear much of his weight. When he got his bearings he took another deep breath. Hank opened up his grow room door and took as many of the hanging plants as he could fit into the duffle bag. It was about twenty-five. He thought that he could fit forty if he had another day to dry them, but it didn't matter. It was all going to produce hash oil anyway.

As he got done putting the premature plants up, he looked around thinking what a waste it was to leave the rest. He sighed deeply, turned and walked out of his grow space forever. As Hank headed back to the stairs he stepped on something. He looked down and saw that it was the doll…Matilda. He began to panic, stumbled backward, bewildered. It hadn't been there a moment before. He tripped over his own duffle bag as he dropped it and fell flat onto his back, scrambling to try to get away from that hellish toy.

Before Hank could sit up a boot came from behind him and put its full weight on his shoulder. He looked up to see Quan standing over him, pinning him to the ground, smiling from ear to ear. Hank screamed as Quan vaporized into a fine blue mist and penetrated every pore of his body, wholly consuming him. Hank was helpless in his own body as the railwayman took control. If Hank could have still cried he would have as he screamed at the possessing spirit in his mind. As even his tear ducts failed him he only had his thoughts to fight the possessing spirit and even those were privy to the wretched thing.

"I ain't done wit' chew yet Hanky buoy. I'm gonna have me some fun," Quan made Hank's lips move and the voice was his own, but his ears dreaded the words he was making.

The first thing Quan did with his body was to walk over to the doll and pick it up off of the floor. Hank could hear Amy on her way up the stairs. She must have heard the screams. She appeared at the top in only another moment, brandishing her shotgun, but only seeing Hank she lowered it immediately.

"Are you alright Hank? I heard screaming!" Amy seemed frantic, which was completely understandable given what they had just been through.

Hank hoped that Quan would just use her for sex the way he had with Amanda Wexler. His hopes were in vain. He knew as soon as his mouth opened again and he heard Quan's words come out.

"Ain't no Hank here girl. Why're you playin' 'round? I thought I done told you not to leave your damn dolls layin' 'round, didn't I?" there was little of Hank left, he could see that in Amy's reaction that she knew it wasn't him. He took a step towards her and backhanded her hard across the mouth, drawing blood. She tried to gather herself, but he was upon her raining blow after blow down on her head and shoulders as she cowered and tried to block what she could.

Quan kicked her and hit her with balled up fists with as much force as he could muster through Hank's body. She was crumpling up, failing to block most of the attacks from landing. Even when she did manage to block him she still suffered horrible pain in her arms. She could tell that he meant to kill her.

Eventually, Quan stopped, unsure if Amy were still alive or not. He stood over her, panting hard through Hank's lungs. Amy heard him turn his attention to the doll and begin speaking to it. She was too dazed to try to pay attention to the words he used, but she knew it was her chance, possibly her only chance to make a dash for the door.

She kicked out at him with both legs, one at the knee Hank had hurt the night before and one at the groin. It knocked Hank down and gave her just enough time to get to the stairs. Hank's hand reached out for her as he got back up, missing her shirt by inches. She spun out of his reach, throwing herself down the stairs frantically, just trying to put distance between them. She was stunned, at the bottom of the stairs, blood pouring into her right eye was making her half blind.

Amy heard the footsteps of the man who was no longer her husband coming down the stairs, slowly, deliberately. She ran to the living room and saw that Hank's shotgun was still there. She wasted no time, snatching up the gun and running back to the stairwell. As Quan poked Hank's head through the door she set upon him with the shotgun, holding it by the barrel and wielding it like a baseball bat. Her first swing hit him square across the jaw, smashing it. She was sure it broke, but she swung again. The second blow hit Hank's body in the shoulder, instantly knocking his whole arm out of socket. She dropped the gun and punched him several times in the face.

"Get out of my fucking husband you motherfucker!" Amy screamed as loud as she could. Then it occurred to her that she needed to get him out of the house. Perhaps removing him from the property would relinquish Hank from the clutches of the spirit that had him.

She grabbed him and pulled him toward the front door. She had always been bigger than he was and usually had twenty pounds on him, but since he was in declining health he had lost quite a bit of weight. Amy was thankful, realizing she would have been battered much more if Hank had been at full weight. As it was she outweighed him by thirty-five pounds and found it easy to drag him through the house once he was stunned. She just hoped that she didn't do any serious damage that couldn't be fixed.

As they got to the porch he found a second wind and began to punch her in the stomach as she carried him. She did her best to ignore it. Amy found that she was through with the situation and would endure whatever she had to to make it end. She threw him down the stairs and he hit the ground hard, bouncing his head off of the concrete walkway to the driveway. She was shocked that she had put so much force into it and she ran down the stairs as fast as she could to begin dragging him toward the car, to get him away from the house, away from the spirit that she was sure was bound to the place, not the person.

When she got to him she waited, clenched fist, to lay him

out. To hopefully knock him unconscious so that she could load him up and they could make their escape. He didn't move. She waited a few more seconds. By then she noticed that there was a steady trickle of blood pouring out of his head, soaking into the ground. She looked up, instinctively looking for someone else to call to for help but all she saw were corpses in black robes strewn about the yard, still lit tiki torches and the scorched earth where the fire had been.

She tried to remain calm and crouched beside him, checking for a pulse. She couldn't find one in his neck. She tried his wrists and couldn't find one in either one. Amy sat down on the bloody ground and began to cry over him. She cried and cried. She cried for so long that she had no idea how many minutes or hours had gone by. Eventually, she gave up. She tried shaking him. She tried praying over him. She tried everything that she could do but to no avail. Amy had killed her husband. She had been trying to protect herself, trying to get him away from the monster that raged inside him and took him over. It was all her fault. Amy was only able to blame herself, as justified as she had felt throwing him down the stairs she knew it wasn't her husband. She should have done more to try to protect him.

Amy got in her car and drove down the driveway, leaving Hank lying face down in the front yard. She didn't look into the rearview once. She could drive away from Gravel Switch Kentucky but she could never drive away from the memory of what she had just done to Hank. The feeling of guilt became a tsunami of suffering as she drove on, just heading west, not even having the slightest clue as to where she was headed. She thought it would be best to stick to the plan and to go to the west coast.

She found the road to be boring and probably the worst

thing for her in the state of mind she was in. Her emotions were totally fractured and she was unable to focus. She almost caused several accidents on the interstate. Realizing she would eventually get pulled over Amy decided to get a hotel room somewhere in Missouri. She had never been there before and didn't plan to stay. So far everything she had seen of the state left her unimpressed. She was happy just to get a bed and sleep. She'd have the entire next day to check out the state and hopefully, find at least something interesting about it.

She found a run down old motel that looked like it had seen much better days. She didn't realize she still had blood on her face, caked on her forehead and her eye until she looked into the mirror to check her self before going in to pay for a room.

There was an old man in a bathrobe and a wife beater tank top shirt at the desk and he was smoking a cigarette and watching old reruns of Barney Miller on an antiquated cathode ray tube television. He ignored Amy even though he had seen her walk in. She stood there for a few moments before passive-aggressively clearing her throat to try to get his attention. He didn't take his eyes off of the television but pointed to a sign on the counter with his cigarette that said For Assistance Please Ring Bell.

"Are you kidding me?" Amy said under her breath, sure the old guy couldn't hear her.

She got a room after a few minutes of dealing with him, although he wouldn't talk to her until she rang the bell, which only let out a dull thud. She found him to be cantankerous and nearly hostile. Amy chalked it up to him being from Missouri. The people must just be rude. She got the room key as quickly as he would give it to her and immediately went to her room, room twenty-two. There wasn't much for furniture, just a chest of drawers with an old television on it and a beat up bed that looked like it probably had bed bugs or lice. She sat down and just tried to collect her thoughts, gather her emotions together and come up with a plan for her life.

Soon she broke into tears that she couldn't control. The weight of what she had done came crashing down on her. She thought of what she had done to Hank in contrast to what he had done to Boris and found sad irony staring back at her. How she had left him when he was sick to be with Jared. She had abandoned Hank when he needed her most.

Wallowing in misery since she no longer had driving to keep her at least a little distracted Amy went out to the car to get some pills and some weed out of the glove box. She was sure that she wanted to get as intoxicated as she could. Amy knew opiates could help with emotional pain just as much as physical. When she opened the car door and went into the glove compartment she saw that she had five or six bottles of pills in it. She grabbed them all indiscriminately and noticed that under all of the bottles was Lief's thirty-eight revolver. She took it too. She never knew what to expect from anyone anymore. She didn't know if she had been followed by any of the cult. She even got so paranoid that she thought that the hotel proprietor was possibly a cult member and she had walked into a trap.

When she got back into the room Amy sat the pills on the bed and the pistol next to them. She pulled a bag of marijuana out of her pocket and some rolling papers. As she began to twist up a joint she noticed that one of the pill bottles was Hank's seizure medication. Another wave of uncontrollable pain overwhelmed her. She felt like her heart was cut out of her chest. There was nothing but a hollow emptiness where it had once been. She thought that she would never love again. She thought that she didn't deserve it.

Amy smoked her joint, taking deep, long pulls off of it. She didn't care what the marijuana laws were in Missouri. She didn't care one bit. If the cops came she could flush the little bit that she had on her person down the toilet. She only hoped that they wouldn't search the car where they had stashed several pounds, to finance their new life wherever they moved.

She sobbed to herself for a few hours, popping pills every twenty minutes or so. The joint she smoked was followed by several more until her small sack of head stash was gone. By the time Amy had smoked all of her weed and eaten so many pills she felt a calmness and numbness like she had been looking for. She decided to take a shower and relax but spent only a few minutes in the bathroom, unable to enter the shower as the room filled with the stench of brimstone; a flashback to her recent horrors overtook her, triggered by the smell that reminded her so much of the ghosts of Gravel Switch. She panicked and fled into the dingy room, not understanding that the motel used well water and that she was smelling sulfur. As she got to the living room, unaware that she was overdosing on an extreme amount of pills, Amy saw two red eyes shining through the blinds. "Have I been too careless? They're here, but I won't let 'em take me!" she thought as she decided to act.

She reached across the bed and grabbed Lief's gun. She held it to her temple, imagining what it would be like to just end it all. To just end up swallowed by darkness and never have to worry about anything again. The longer Amy thought of it the more she liked the idea. Amy even considered that she might see Hank again if she did pull the trigger. The thought wasn't abhorrent to her at all. She held the pistol there for what seemed to her to be a long time, where she considered the fate of her soul itself. But it had only been the briefest of moments before she made her choice. She wasn't going to let the demon take her.

"I'm coming Haaaannk! " Amy screamed just before she pulled the trigger. She never heard the sound of the revolver as the bullet exploded out of the chamber and tore through the side of her head in an eruption of brains and skull fragments, splattering the wall behind her. The tail lights of the truck right outside her window illuminated the dripping gore with a red glow.

THE HARVEST

*H*ank awoke on the ground in his front yard with the worst headache he had ever felt to find that it was dark out. He saw that he was in a pool of his own blood. It was a few minutes before he could even sit up. When he did he saw that his front yard was empty of any corpses. The only sign that anything had happened at the property at all was the black spot on the ground, the remains of the bonfire pit. Hank stood up and wiped his hands on his pants. Things weren't too clear to him. He was uncertain why he was in the yard, wondering if he had suffered a seizure. He had no idea how long he had been there, but could tell by the position of the moon in the sky that it was not late at night but already early the next morning.

He took a few deep breaths and noticed that Amy's car was gone. He was alone at the house which panicked him a bit after the night before. It was several minutes until Hank got his head straight enough to think of what to do next. He decided to go inside and get his cell phone and call somebody to come get him. Part of him just wanted to get up and walk out of town, maybe hitchhike to Lexington.

As he approached the house he saw that the front door was open and the doll Matilda was lying there, just inside the door. He bent down to pick up the doll and as soon as he touched it everything came back to him. Everything he had done when Quan had seized control of him. He even remembered Amy trying to wake him up, checking his pulse and deciding he was dead.

He dropped the doll and recoiled from it, ran into the house and got his phone out of the bedroom. He tried to call Amy but repeatedly got her voice mail. He left message after message explaining that he was sorry for what Quan had made him do. He kept getting a gnawing feeling in the pit of his stomach that he could not shake. A feeling that something was very, very wrong.

A few minutes into trying to call Amy he got a call himself. It was from a county sheriff's office in Missouri. He would normally never answer such a call, but under the circumstances, he figured that it was best to do so. He figured that it might have something to do with Amy. He answered with a plain, "Hello", as his heart sank. The feeling that something was just horribly wrong swelled in his chest.

"Mister Ramsey?" the voice on the other end sounded semi-robotic.

"Uh huh. That's me," Hank started to tremble.

"Mister Ramsey this is deputy sheriff Larson with the Jefferson County sheriff's department in Missouri. Sir, I regret to inform you that your wife Amy has taken her own life. She shot herself at a motel this morning. I'm sorry for your loss," the sheriff delivered the news emotionlessly. Hank wondered if the officer actually was a robot as he dropped the phone and fell to his knees, clutching at the ground and wailing in emotional agony from the devastating news.

The sheriff stayed on the other end for a few minutes, but Hank paid him no attention. Hank couldn't even hear the man talking over his own miserable sobbing and gasping. He felt like his own heart had been torn out. He had driven her to such lengths that she thought that she had killed him and in her own desperate emotional state had shot herself. He let the thought sink in, but knew the weight of the emotional magnitude would be a surreal thing that would slowly consume and envelope him entirely.

He flew into a rage, jumping up quickly and rushing through the house to the stairs. He went up them and got the shotgun Amy had left up there when she came to see if he was alright; when Quan had taken him and he had attacked her. He went to his room and found some shells and walked back to the front porch, picking up the doll Matilda on the way.

He threw the doll high into the air into the yard and raised the shotgun, fired and decimated the rotten thing. The buckshot smashed her head apart and tore through what was left of the fabric of her dress. He fired the other barrel at hit her again as she lay on the ground. Hank walked over to the doll and shot her until he was out of shells.

Still fuming he began to smash what was left of her head with the butt of the shotgun. He then grabbed her and tore at her clothes with his bare hands, trying to shred her last tattered bits to nothing. When he was satisfied that it could never be repaired in any way Hank scooped up the pieces. He carried the shattered parts down his driveway, walked out to the road and headed for Bernice Hickman's house.

It was quite a long walk in the state of mind he was in. He didn't even know what to say to her, he just wanted to get the doll as far away from him as he could and to show Bernice that he had destroyed it. Even after everything, it was the doll that he loathed the most. More than Alan, more than Jared. More than anything he could think of Hank despised the doll.

When he got to Bernice's house Hank was happy to see that she was home. It was s short driveway up to a house twice as big as the one she had been renting him. It was a veritable mansion. In its day it must have been quite a luxurious home, but its day had come and gone over a hundred and fifty years before. She was sitting on the porch, smoking a cigar and sipping moonshine from a mason jar. It didn't occur to him that she was already drinking heavily that early in the morning.

"I have your damn doll, Bernie! I want you to have it back!" he was still furious and tried to carry that energy with him. He tried to deliver some sort of righteousness with his words that she obviously failed to recognize.

"I see that you didn't take good care of her Hank," Bernice said as Hank approached. She had a wry smile on her face. "Well, her soul is at peace now at least."

He got to the bottom of the porch and threw the doll parts and tattered fabric, some of which was essentially just powder and dust, at the feet of his landlord. Hank didn't know what to say, he didn't know what to do. He only knew he was hurting inside so badly that he couldn't take it. He turned his back and began to walk away when Bernice stopped him with a loud whistle, the kind one would use to call a dog or a horse. He stopped in his tracks.

"Come on, sit down Hank. Let's smoke a joint. Have a sip of 'shine. I'm sorry to hear about Amy," Hank gave her a puzzled look as she revealed that she knew about Amy's demise. "Oh, yeah. I have the same gift as Phyllis did. Not as strong…

but I have it too. I felt her presence leave this plane as soon as she was gone."

Hank looked puzzled but sat down to have a smoke and a drink anyway. He didn't care. What did he have to lose? Amy was gone, the house was gone. The grow was gone. Amy had taken the money and the crop. Every single thing they harvested and saved up to make their move to California or Washington was gone. Every dollar he had was gone. He was broke, desolate, homeless and a widower. Hank couldn't get any more broken than he was, by his own reckoning.

He sat quietly on the top step of the porch and took a gulping drink off of the moonshine, oblivious to the fact that it seared his throat and tongue. He set the jar down and made a beckoning motion for her to pass him the joint she had just lit. She giggled a little at his impatience.

They sat there until the afternoon had come and smoked and drank themselves half stupid. Hank wondered why she was being so kind to him, considering everything that had happened, he was still unsure where she fit into it all. She didn't seem to mind one bit that he had destroyed her doll. If he should even think of it in such terms he was unsure. It was definitely its own entity, its own presence. Hank found himself considering that perhaps she didn't own it. Perhaps it owned her.

The fall afternoon was cold and after an entire morning of drinking and smoking, Bernie found that she was hungry and offered Hank some reheated pot pie that her mother had made the night before. He accepted her offer and within a few minutes, she had come back with a steaming hot plate for him that she admitted to being embarrassed for microwaving.

He didn't care a bit if it were microwaved or not and scarfed it down quickly and easily, burping loud in satisfaction when he was done. Bernice was not even halfway done with the equally sized plate that she had fixed for herself. She handed him a bag of marijuana to roll an after lunch joint as she finished her plate.

He rolled it but before he got it lit Hank began to feel light headed and tired. His vision got blurry and not just from the moonshine. He knew immediately that she had drugged him but was unable to do anything about it. He collapsed to the ground, paralyzed yet aware of everything that was happening. His entire body refused to move. All that he could manage to make work were his eyes. He lay there, completely helpless and under her power. Bernice could do anything she wanted to Hank and there was nothing he could do to stop her.

As she stood up and approached him, smacking her lips as she stood over him, Alan emerged from her front door. He walked out on the porch and put his arm around Bernice saying, "Look here cousin. We got us a bountiful harvest to reap this fall, now don't we? I ain't seen a crop like 'is one in years. The buoy don't even know what he did when he smashed up Matilda does he?"

Hank was flabbergasted. He knew that whatever they had planned for him wasn't good. Alan walked over to Bernice's truck and produced a heavy dog chain from the behind the seat. He tied one end around Hank's feet and the other he fixed to the bumper hitch.

Hank couldn't scream but he could still feel what was going on. They drug him slowly down the road, leaving twenty feet of slack in the chain. It began as pure unadulterated agony. The road was both a cheese grater and sandpaper slowly peeling his skin off with tiny chunks of gravel and bits of debris. It ate through his clothes quickly. They stopped every thirty seconds to a minute to make sure he was still alive. They made the short drive to his house a half hour hell ride. Every second torture. Every moment he begged to die so that his anguish could end.

Hank clung to the edge of life, fading in and out of consciousness by the time that they got to the house where he had lived for so long. All of the skin and much of the flesh of his back was gone. All that remained was a bloody mess. There were rib bones visible on his back when they unchained him and Alan was quite surprised to see that Hank still clung to life.

Alan picked Hank up like a groom carrying a bride and took him over the threshold of the house, into the foyer, then sat him on a chair under the chandelier. Hank faded in and out of consciousness, only aware that he knew pain and it was his inseparable, conjoined twin. He had become so intertwined with pain that he knew nothing else. Even his own name eluded him. He wasn't even sure if he were still being dragged down the road or not. Out of nowhere, a memory flashed through his mind of the first time he had come to Marion County Kentucky. A memory of a man with a very thick hillbilly accent telling him, "The reason they call it Gravel Switch is cuz that's where the road switches to gravel." That would be Hank's last reminiscence. A vague recollection of a time that seemed long ago.

Unaware of who or what he was, had been or had become, Hank was oblivious when Alan put the chain around his neck. Bernice came back into the house, she splashed Hank in the face with moonshine. It stung him badly, exacerbating the already excruciating, transcendental pain. Hank's eyes opened, empty and seemingly void of any awareness.

Bernice stripped off her clothes and began to paint on her flesh with Hank's blood after she wiped her hand across his back, snapping him back into consciousness. Still too dazed by the pain to comprehend what he was seeing Hank just wanted to let go, just wanted to die. But the pain itself kept him in his mortal coil. Alan came back into his view and injected him with some sort of drug. Then there was darkness.

*H*ank came to and found that he was extremely intoxicated. He knew the high, it was heroin. He also knew that it was all that was keeping him alive. Hank didn't know how long he had been out, but he knew it couldn't have been long; he didn't have that much blood left to shed. He saw that he was in a chair, with the dog chain around his neck. There were arcane, occult symbols drawn on the walls in his blood. Bernice was nude, she had painted the same symbols all over her body in his blood that were on the walls. She was on all fours, naked, facing Hank and speaking in the same strange tongue that Jared had spoken in as the high priest. Alan was behind her, groaning in pleasure as he thrust himself into her. Hank's awareness had returned just enough for him to realize that he was seeing a sex magic ritual and not just watching two people screw.

Alan had an orgasm eventually and he stared Hank directly in the eyes as it overtook him. When he was done Bernice stood up and declared, "It is time."

Alan got to his feet as well. Hank was still completely paralyzed. Powerless. He knew what her words meant. He knew he was not long for this world. That was the only solace that he had left.

Alan went into another room and came back in a moment. He had a large, industrial-sized container of salt. He poured a triangle of salt around Hank, followed by other curvilinear shapes that Hank neither recognized nor could focus on. Hank became aware of blue, vaporous, amorphous shapes. Vaguely human they loomed all about him, outside of the triangle, on the edges of it, but not within it. He became aware that they were there for him. They were there to take him. His essence would fade from his body and he would be one of them. Trapped forever in the house like all the other ghosts. At that final moment, Hank knew what it had all been about. He knew that his destiny had always been to suffer horribly and be sacrificed to the house. To whatever demon that the structure was a front for. He began to chuckle to himself. He knew that the Hickman's and Alan Fox were just as much fools as Jared was. In their hubris, they would try to command powers that they could not comprehend.

Hank felt a strong tugging on his neck and became aware that he was being lifted into the air by the chain. Alan and Bernice were working in unison to hoist him up. It took time and Bernice positioned the chair under him so that he was standing on it, or more like flopping on it as he was finally strung up to the chandelier.

There was another round of chanting in weird tongues and Hank would have laughed, had he been able to, at how obligatory it seemed. How trite. They thought that they were buying power from beyond the veil. They thought they were offering him up as a harvest to their demon lord. A dark offering to appease a dark master. He knew what he would become and he welcomed it. He had a bone to pick with Quan anyway and he wanted to settle that score sooner than later, even though he would have all of eternity to do so.

He smelled cannabis. They had lit a joint up as they were about to off him! He couldn't believe it and in an extreme use of his last willpower, he puckered his lips a few times, letting them know that he wanted to hit the joint too. Alan laughed as he held Hank up by the legs, making sure that he didn't collapse and hang himself until they were ready. Alan knew the paralysis would be wearing off, but Hank was nowhere near able to stand on his own.

Bernice noticed that Alan was completely uncaring and although they had a job to do together in sacrificing her tenant it wasn't in her nature to deny a dying man his final wish. She let Alan know he was being an ass by the tone in her voice as she said, "It's the least that we can do, Alan. The poor kid has suffered enough, soon he'll be our Lord's forever. Let's give him this one last thing. Put the joint in his mouth." Bernice had decided to show the tiniest bit of compassion and Hank was quite thankful.

Alan put the joint up to Hank's lips and he pulled a deep toke off of it. Exhaling he managed the tiniest nod to let Alan know that he wanted another. After five tokes Alan and Bernice were both at the end of their compassion. Alan stomped the roach out on the hardwood floor. Hank could see the vaporous figures much more clearly, especially when a cloud of the marijuana smoke rolled over one. Then he could see their features clearly, see them for who they were. The little girl in the white dress came forward, into the triangle of magical sigils and protective signs, throwing Hank off guard. She took his hand as Alan kicked the chair out from under Hank.

Hank Ramsey fell from the chair, snapping his already lacerated neck. He choked to death slowly as he spasmed. His eyes bulged out of his head as he gasped involuntarily. As his bowels emptied and the last beats that his heart would ever beat rang inside his chest and pounded in his ears Hank let go of all the pain and suffering and succumbed to death. He walked willingly into her cold embrace, not struggling against her nor trying to flee. He wished that death were his final destination, he found the void to be such a peaceful place. The darkness, the nothingness, the nonexistence was a pure peace he had never once in his life known. As his consciousness faded to black he knew only a deep serenity.

The peace of death lasted but a mere moment as he was snatched by grasping talons and pulled through a tunnel of spiraling light and darkness. The shock of being torn through dimensions, of being given a consciousness again with which to perceive, was a tornado of sensation. Everything he had ever done in his life, everything he had ever felt, all occurring contemporaneously. Then there was a calm, the eye of the storm that he was passing through. The spirit awoke to find himself in the foyer of his house, again the identity of Hank Ramsey was the mantle he wore, although he understood he was now a spectral being; at least to some extent. Hank had suspected that he would end up like Quan and Sheridan and all the others, but there was nothing he could have done to prepare himself for staring at his own corpse hanging from the chandelier.

Sweet oblivion was gone.

EPILOGUE

"Hi, Lester. How've you been? You know you are my favorite uncle don't you?" Bernice spoke loudly into her cell phone, knowing that her great uncle was getting hard of hearing.

"Oh, I'm just fine dear. Just callin' to let you know that we found you some new tenants. They don't smell quite as good as them last ones we found you, but they'll do just fine," the old man spoke jovially, happy to hear the voice of his great niece.

"You weren't kiddin' about that last one. He sure was somethin' special. We had a great harvest, me and your grandson Alan took care of everything," Bernice assured him.

"Jared almost fucked everything up for all of us. But these past few years have been full of bounty since we had that sweet harvest," the old man smacked his lips as if licking barbecue sauce off of his fingers and savoring the tanginess.

"Oh, yeah. He took it upon himself to try to force the infinite to his own twisted will. He dared to command our Lord when he should have been on his knees. He deserved everything he got. Still, seeing that much power come through. Our Lord may not come for many more lifetimes, but he blessed us with a glimpse of his..." the words for what she had seen when the veil between dimensions had lifted eluded her.

"I remember dear. I remember. It was a blessing to us all. Ia Shub-Niggurath!" the old man was excited remembering that night when they had seen their god.

"Okay uncle Lester, I'm gonna go now. It was good to talk to you. I expect the new tenants will be calling me tomorrow?"

"They sure will dear. You take care of yourself. Tell Alan and the twins I said hi. How old are they now? Ten?"

"No uncle Lester, they're twelve now, believe it or not. Oh, one last thing. Do you think I should bother putting a new roof on the house?" she asked, genuinely concerned.

"If you have the money, well, I'd do it. But don't do it for any renters. Hell, they probably ain't gonna be around too long anyways," the old man laughed a cantankerous cackle at the thought of feeding the young couple he had met earlier that day to the house. To his dark, demon-god.

"That's what I was thinking uncle Lester. That's what I was thinking. Tell aunt Betty that I said hi," Bernice said, feeling awkward that she had forgotten her aunt.

"I will dear. When she gets in from the toolshed. She's out there breakin' in our new pet. Some yuppie from San Francisco. I don't know how the hell he ended up out here, but we've had him about two weeks now. Betty just loves him to death, but I don't know. He kinda smells like cheese farts to me!" the old man guffawed so hard he began to choke a little and went into a deep coughing fit before hanging up the phone.

The next day she got a call from a Louisville number. The number of the young couple that were looking to rent a serene place out in the country. They left a long voicemail and Bernice could tell by the sounds of their voices that she would have another great harvest very soon.

"Hi, this is Bernice Hickman and I'm returning your call about my house for rent.

Yes. Gravel Switch. Uh-huh. It's four hundred and fifty dollars a month. Ok then. Sure. See you tomorrow…"

AFTERWORD

Writing Gravel switch was one hell of a ride. It was three years after my best friend died and his wife killed herself and I was still finding that I was unable to cope with my feelings about it. Rather than write a book based on the true story, which is scary enough on its own, I chose to write a fictionalized account of their deaths. In doing so I tried to produce a story very much like the sort of B grade horror movies that Hank was so fond of. I tried to keep the feel fast paced and never take the story too seriously. Creating fictional characters loosely based on real, albeit deceased, people was quite a fun challenge. It was also emotionally draining in a very masochistic way.

I was inspired to write Gravel Switch as an amalgamation of the truth, which is itself extreme and hard to believe, and those kind of horror stories like Evil Dead and Creepshow. When reality is so over the top then the art that pays homage to it should itself be over the top.

-Aleister

ACKNOWLEDGMENTS

I would like to acknowledge that without the encouragement of my dad and the patience of my wife I would not have been able to write this book. Thank you both, from the bottom of my heart.

A special thanks to H.P. Lovecraft for creating the mythos that so many of us write stories in. What a beast you unleashed!

Gary Gygax will always have my undying gratitude for showing me at such a young age that imagination is without limits.

I would like to thank my dear friends who allowed me to use their own real life experiences in Gravel Switch as a catalyst to do horrific things to them in this book. I had a great time torturing you guys!

Finally I would like to thank Henry and Annette. Without your tragic deaths under such extreme circumstances I would not have been inspired to write Gravel Switch. May you Rest In Peace.

ABOUT THE AUTHOR

Born in Lexington Kentucky and living in Oakland California for the past twenty years Aleister Davidson is a writer of horror, science fiction and fantasy stories. Preferring to keep his themes weird he loves cosmic, Lovecraftian elements. He is a guitarist who has been playing since 1983, but steadily since 1986. A master of several genres from punk to jazz, funk to metal he brings an eclectic flavor to his writing that is reminiscent of his music. Although primarily a horror and science fiction author Aleister's main influences are George Orwell, Douglas Adams, Kurt Vonnegut, Michael Moorcock, H.P. Lovecraft and Robert E. Howard.

Aleister is a proud Oaklander and lives a quiet life in the hills with his wife. He loves cats.

For more information visit the author's website below. While you are there make sure sign up for his email list for news about upcoming releases and the occasional free short story.

www.aleisterdavidson.com
aleisterdavidson@blackmantispress.com

THANK YOU FOR READING!

If you liked the book please take a moment to leave a review on Amazon and/or Goodreads.

Reviews help authors a great deal and are always greatly appreciated.

www.ingramcontent.com/pod-product-compliance
Lightning Source LLC
Chambersburg PA
CBHW030251200626
46816CB00002BA/603